Anonymous

The Ladye Nancye

Vol. II

Anonymous

The Ladye Nancye
Vol. II

ISBN/EAN: 9783337053192

Printed in Europe, USA, Canada, Australia, Japan

Cover: Foto ©Andreas Hilbeck / pixelio.de

More available books at **www.hansebooks.com**

𝔄 𝔑𝔬𝔳𝔢𝔩.

BY

THE AUTHOR OF

'DAME DURDEN,' 'MY LORD CONCEIT'
'DARBY AND JOAN,'

ETC., ETC.

IN THREE VOLUMES.

VOL. II.

LONDON:
WARD AND DOWNEY,
12, YORK STREET, COVENT GARDEN, W.C.
1887.

CONTENTS OF VOL. II.

BOOK III.—*Continued.*

'THE LADYE NANCYE.'

BOOK III.—*Continued.*
PENANCE.

CHAPTER VIII.

WE all walked home in the cool summer dusk.

The old Frenchman, and I, and Nancette in front, the boys and Mdlle. Léonie behind. The old man was a courteous and intelligent companion. I liked his formal phrases, his polite speeches, and gracefully-turned compliments. I began to think that French people had a knack of putting you on good terms with yourself that their insular neighbours could never acquire.

He and I had most of the conversation to ourselves. Nancette was silent and self-absorbed. I knew she was brooding over her discovery. It was annoying and perplexing. I could only hope that the scapegrace son would keep out of the way. There certainly was nothing in this remote and quiet little place to tempt a worldly and dissolute man to visit it, unless, of course, he heard of Nancette's presence here.

I felt that Fate had played us a scurvy trick. The peace and enjoyment of our visit were threatened by a new catastrophe. When we parted with our new friends, which was close to our own domicile, I felt it incumbent on me to say I hoped for the pleasure of future meetings, but I fear the speech was not so sincere as it might have been, or would have been, but for that whisper of Nancette's as she stood beside me on the cliff.

After our simple supper was over, and the

boys had gone to bed, Nancette and I went out into the garden. It was all dusk and dim, save for the light of the young June moon, showing clearly in the purple-blue of the sky. Delicious scents of roses, and lilies, and heliotrope, and verbena reached us from every nook and corner of the fragrant wilderness. We paced up and down, silent at first, but gradually giving vent to thoughts that we instinctively guessed were shared, even if unspoken.

'Do you think there is any chance of his coming here?' I asked hesitatingly.

'No,' she said almost sternly; 'he has been a bad son. It is for his sake that poor old man has to work so hard for his living. He told me he had not seen him for years.'

'And you,' I said. 'Did you tell him anything?'

She shook her head.

'No, I could not.'

17—2

'But he is a relative of yours ?' I said.

'Yes, my grand-uncle. But as he has chosen to hide his name for many, many years, I do not like to claim relationship. My father was not on good terms with him when he was young.'

'How did he betray his identity?' I asked.

'It escaped him accidentally; he was talking of some place in Normandy where he used to live.'

'It is unfortunate,' I said, 'this meeting. Supposing Pierre de Volens did come here ?'

'I think I should be able to meet him as Pierre de Volens,' she said.

I looked at her. Her face was turned seawards. I could only see the soft, sad curve of mouth and chin.

'I am glad to hear it,' I said. 'But we cannot measure our force of resistance until we are tried.'

'There is no resurrection,' she said, 'for a

love that has died the death of unworthiness. Every day I live tells me that.'

'You are quite right,' I answered. 'But how have you learnt the lesson?'

'From you, I think,' she said, with a sudden glance at my face. 'And partly from my own researches. You don't know —you can't imagine how different things look to me now to what they did even a year ago. Am I fickle, do you think?'

'Far from it,' I said quickly; 'you are only wise. I cannot understand a woman loving a man whose every action proclaims him selfish, mean, trivial and dishonourable. I mean continuing to love him—wrecking life, honour, and future for his sake. The whole course of conduct pursued by Pierre de Volens has shown him to be a contemptible and worthless man. If you will look at his behaviour to you by the light of reason and common-sense—not of passion and devotion—you will see I am right.'

'I know you are right,' she said with a faint sigh, 'and I do not shrink from meeting him.'

'Has his power over you really evaporated?' I asked. 'Do not be too sure. If he stood here now—this moment—could you greet him without a rush of the old overmastering feeling—the throb of pulse and heart — the agony of remembrance that dignifies even trifles?'

'Yes,' she said quite calmly, 'I could. I told you something had gone out of my very heart that day by the sea. Nothing he could do or say would ever bring it back —nothing. It was the end for me.'

'But supposing,' I said, 'it were not the end for—him? Supposing he should persecute you again? You see I do not dignify his love by any very grand title. Supposing he should appeal to you by the memory of that youthful love; that—that secret you share--what then?'

She shivered a little, as if a breath of fear had touched her.

'It would not alter me now,' she said. 'I seem to have grown cold and hard to every memory. There are a hundred things —mean, false, and paltry—that have come back to me' stripped of their glamour, and they all say the same thing. Ah, if I had only been wise enough to believe my father's words.'

'It is better to be wise late than never,' I said. 'If it is final, as you think, I do not see what you have to fear. All the same, I hope it may not occur to M. Pierre to pay his father a visit. I wonder what he has been doing these last eighteen months?'

'More things to regret than to be proud of, perhaps,' said Nancette sadly. 'Sometimes I feel sorry for the girl who had such grand and perfect dreams of her hero. A hero,' she laughed bitterly, 'who powdered his face and curled his hair, and was only a sawdust doll after all !'

' I am glad you discovered that in time,' I said. ' Women's greatest fault is that they will idealize men. It is such a mistake. Then the day of disillusion comes, and with it comes bitterness, hatred, despair ! I sometimes think it is better to strike too low a key than too high a one. The disappointment has a chance of being the other way.'

She sighed again. Her eyes went out to the calm sea and the rippling line of silver left by the moonlight.

' Doesn't it seem a little sad,' she said, ' to gaze on such a scene alone ? Don't you feel a longing for love and comprehension— for something that is not an aimless dream ? When you touch a chord there is an echo——'

' Yes,' I said as she paused, her eyes wide and pained in their straining, passionate gaze.

'But the echo can never be caught or held. It is sweet and clear, but no more tangible than the longings that fill a woman's heart, and which, for want of a better word, the world calls romance. It is subtle,' she said, 'and dangerous.'

'A cynic once said that at seventeen a woman is in love with love; at twenty, with her lover; at thirty, with herself. You, my dear, should be only in the first stage.'

'Love! love! love! Always the same story!' she said impatiently. 'I wonder if it is an experience of every life?'

'I fancy so,' I answered. 'No exception has been chronicled. Sooner or later, every man or woman loves wisely, or foolishly. It is a law of nature.'

She turned to me and laid her hand on my arm caressingly.

'I wonder,' she said, 'whom you loved? Was he good, noble, clever? He ought to have been.'

' I am very susceptible to flattery,' I said with a light laugh. ' He was, of course, all that; otherwise, I could not have loved him.'

' Then,' she said anxiously, ' you were happy ?'

' Naturally,' I said. ' With such a hero, could I help being in a state of bliss ?'

' And did it last ? I mean—— Oh, Myra, I beg your pardon, I forgot. But at least you are happy in a memory so noble and true.'

' Yes,' I said, somewhat unsteadily ; ' it is something to have a memory to worship, considering that women must have some sort of an idol. Even if they are broken, we keep the bits—just as in our childish days we kept our dolls' broken limbs. No wonder men can't understand us !'

' Nor we them,' she said with another sigh.

' Which is one good and sufficient reason

for patience and toleration in married life. It ought to be specified in the service.'

'Your married life did not show that,' she said, looking at me in the clear pale moonlight; 'you confessed as much. You were singularly fortunate.'

'My married life?' A red flush rose to my cheeks. 'I never spoke of it to you,' I said—' nor to anyone,' I added bitterly.

She looked puzzled.

'Was not that—that hero of yours, your husband?' she asked.

I hesitated, but those frank, compelling eyes seemed to force the truth from me despite myself.

'No,' I said; 'it was someone I knew long—long ago.'

'But not your husband. And yet you married?'

'That was my sin,' I said, 'and my punishment. Believe me, I am not the

only woman who has proved cause and effect
in a similar manner.'

'It seems very sad,' she said ; ' very sad !'

'Oh,' I cried with sudden unreasoning
passion, 'is not all life sad ? You begin it
so hopefully—you think everything is to
come ; then in a few years you find nothing
is to come. You would like to sit with
veiled eyes and weep over all that is false,
and fickle, and heart-breaking, but you can't
even do that.   Life pushes you on—on, re-
morselessly to the end—the bitter end of the
grave.   Then you are forgotten, poor little
unit in the vast sum of humanity.   Your
place is filled—the place that seemed to you
so all-important here ; and then a voice may
speak pityingly or disparagingly your name,
and that is all.'

'It is not like you to be so bitter,' she
said gently. 'I scarcely recognise you in
such a mood.'

'I scarcely recognise myself,' I said with

an effort. 'Perhaps we are but hypocrites after all—even to ourselves. That solves the mystery, does it not?'

She shook her head.

'You are no hypocrite,' she said softly; 'but I think you are a woman who has loved and suffered.'

'You are right,' I said, with so near a tendency to emotion that it frightened me for my cherished self-command.

'Do not let us drift into pathos,' I went on, 'or personality. Moonlight and sentiment are dangerous things for women whose lives are lonely, whose hearts are young. We are safer, and wiser too, in the sunlight and with the boys.'

She smiled somewhat wistfully.

'No doubt you are right,' she said; 'let us be prosaic, and go indoors.'

On the table in the little sitting-room a white packet gleamed. I took it up. It was in old Deborah's handwriting. An enclosure fell out—a foreign letter. I knew the writing at a glance.

‘ It is from Errol !’ I exclaimed.

She grew very white. She stood near me as I read it. I seemed to see the strained anxiety of look and attitude. The letter was very brief. As I laid it down I met her glance.

‘ Is he coming home ?’ she asked eagerly.

I shook my head.

‘ No,’ I said. ‘ He is as obdurate as ever. Will you read it ?’ handing her the letter.

‘ No,’ she said, with sudden passion; ‘ it is not to me, nor meant for me. Why should I ?’

Then she left the room. I gathered up the letters and folded them together.

‘ The ice is melting,’ I said to myself. ‘ She grows jealous and resentful, instead of indifferent. Who can fathom the contradictions of a woman's nature ?’

CHAPTER IX.

It does not take one very long to know Guernsey. In two weeks we seemed quite familiar with the wild coast, the pretty tiny bays, and the lovely little water-lanes. We had made excursions to the fort, to L'Ancresse Common, to St. Peter's Valley, and the old castle and church. But the lanes were our favourite resort. They were so cool and shaded, so picturesque and delightful, in these hot summer days, with the drip of water from the rocks, and their great spreading ferns, and thick-leaved trees, and the breaks through which one caught the gleam of sea, or islet, or cliff, like a bright surprise of sapphire and sunlight.

We paid visits to the market, and listened

to the odd dialect of the country-folk, and made incomprehensible bargains with them for fruit and vegetables. We also went into foolish ecstasies over the orchids, and ixias, and sea-stock, so novel in their natural growing state to our English eyes. We recklessly plundered ferns, and wild flowers, and the curious horned poppies, and beautified and decorated our cottage parlour with these spoils. We discovered that the magnolia was a tree, not a shrub, and that the myrtle could spread itself over house-walls so lavishly, that its height was only limited by the roofs.

Every day was occupied; every hour was idly pleasant, or pleasantly idle. We went a good deal on the water, being all of us excellent sailors. We made excursions to Herm, with its pretty stretch of sands, and to Sark, that Basil declared ought to be named Mahomet's Coffin, because it always looked suspended between sea and sky; and we

grew very friendly with M. Jean, and en-
joyed his courteous, clever talk as much as
Léonie's sharp little speeches.

It has done Nancette good to be drawn
out of herself and her morbid griefs, and
to pass these long sunny days in the glorious
air and sunlight, and cheerful companionship
of that youthful trio. For the girl and the
two boys are always with her when possible.
I have to make company for M. St. Jean.
I jot down little fragments in my journal to
tell of how the days go. They are very
uneventful, but very pleasant; and as one
follows another my dread of a catastrophe
lessens. Nancette's name conveys nothing
to M. St. Jean. He calls her 'Madame
Nancye,' in preference to her long, hard
marriage-name, and Léonie does the same.

It is still a mystery to me who Léonie
is. I have heard of no son or daughter with
the exception of the mysterious son in Paris,
who has been such a source of trouble and

anxiety to the old man. I often wonder if Léonie is the daughter of Pierre de Volens, or if Pierre de Volens had a wife at some period or other of his life. I have heard Léonie say that her mother died years ago when she was a small infant, and she seems to have no recollection of any other home save this with the old people.

Madame St. Jean is a taciturn, grim old lady, highly religious, and with a strong prejudice in favour of convents that neither her husband nor Léonie shares—happily for the latter. It is hardly necessary to say that our excursions are not countenanced or accompanied by her.

Something occurred to-day that has greatly puzzled me. We were all walking up the steep harbour road, when we saw in advance of us a stout womanly figure toiling along in the hot sunshine.

We soon overtook her, and as Nancette

passed I observed her glance round in curiosity. Then, to my surprise, she uttered a quick, sharp exclamation, and stood there gazing at the woman as if terrified.

The woman looked with equal astonishment at Nancette. She was a dark, stout Frenchwoman of some forty or forty-five years, I should imagine.

She advanced and said something in a low voice. Nancette signed to Léonie and the boys to walk on with me, and then stayed behind talking to the woman for some four or five minutes.

Then she rejoined us, looking pale and disturbed.

' Who was your friend ?' asked Basil, laughing. ' Rum-looking old party. Wish she'd give me her recipe for moustaches.'

' She is some one I knew in London,' said Nancette ; ' a French lady.'

' You don't say so !' exclaimed Basil ironically. ' We should all have taken her for English. We are very much wiser now.'

The girl looked at him, half perplexed, half sorrowful.

'Do not tease,' she said. 'I can't tell you more about her.'

'Well, so long as she is neither near nor dear to you, we will excuse your reticence,' he said lightly. 'We were afraid she might constitute herself your chaperon.'

But Nancette did not smile, nor did the troubled look leave her face. Presently the boys went on with Léonie. We heard them laughing and jesting in their usual fashion.

'What has troubled you?' I asked Nancette. 'You look so changed.'

'Do I?' she said, as she pushed back the hair off her forehead with a tired little gesture. 'I dare say. That meeting was so unexpected. It brought back things I had almost forgotten.'

'That woman—is she a friend, really?' I asked.

'A friend!' She looked round. Her face was white and scared; her lips trembled. 'Did I call her that?' she faltered. 'I should have said the worst enemy my life has ever known. It would have been nearer the truth. Don't look at me like that, Myra, and, oh, don't ask me more! I can't tell you —I can't tell anyone.'

'My dear,' I said, 'tell me nothing that you do not wish. I am only sorry that a chance meeting has been able to spoil your pleasure here.'

She clasped her hands together passionately; a strange white line came round her close-set lips.

'I am never to know any pleasure—any peace,' she said in a strange, hurried way. 'Fate is against me. The moment I begin to forget, to enjoy, to feel a little light of heart, a little hopeful, then something or some one appears, and it is all spoilt.'

I was silent. I could only look compassion-
ately at the flushed misery of her face.   I
did not care to utter commonplace conso-
lation.

We reached the shady winding road leading
to our domicile. The cool shade was delicious
after the hot glare of the sun.   Insects were
humming in the dry, short grass ; the leaves
were swaying in a lazy, indolent fashion ; the
clear treble of a lark's song thrilled suddenly
from the sea-blue vault of sky above us.   She
paused and looked up.

'Oh,' she cried below her breath, 'if it
were only possible to shake off earth, and its
memories, and necessities, and pains, and take
flight like that !'

'It is not possible,' I said, ' and you must '
try to learn that.   A few years hence—who
knows ?—you may feel very glad that your
wish had not wings.'

'A few years hence.'   She smiled a little
bitter smile. 'You credit me with too much

fortitude,' she said. 'I could not live through many years such as this last has been.'

And as I looked at the delicate, wistful face a thrill of fear touched me. I felt that the isolation and suffering of her secret-burdened life might indeed be too much for her to bear.

'Do not say such things,' I entreated. 'We are not tried beyond our strength. We see that when we look back——'

'Oh,' she said with a shudder, 'do not say more! Before one can look back, think how much one may have to live through. It is that—that fear, that saps all my strength.'

So this day, begun so well and cheerily, is on its way to join the memory of other days. I have not seen Nancette since the morning. She went to her room, and excused herself from joining us again on the plea of severe headache.

I have passed the evening writing up my

journal and despatching a brief account of our
journey here to Errol Glendenning. His last
letter to me was from Mexico. Why, in the
name of everything wild and improbable, he
had gone there I cannot imagine.

In writing, I once more urged upon him
the folly of his conduct, the strange slur cast
upon his wife and home, the more than
certainty that rumour and speculation would
set all sorts of stories afloat to his own and
his wife's discredit. I also told him that her
health was far from strong, that unhappiness
was sapping the springs of youth and hope,
and all that her fair young years should
know. But even as I wrote I felt how hopeless my entreaties were, and was more inclined to tear up the letter than to send
it.

When I had finished writing I went out
into the garden. It was quite deserted. The
boys had gone off somewhere on their own

account. I walked slowly to and fro in the soft dusk. My mind was busy and pre-occupied. I came at last to the gates, and stood looking out on the white, stony road in an absent fashion. Presently I heard voices. They were loud and angry, apparently raised in some discussion. They were speaking in French, but too rapidly and excitedly for me to follow.

I drew back a little into the shade. The speakers passed the gates. I saw them distinctly. One was the stout, swarthy-faced Frenchwoman who had spoken to Nancette ; the other was a man. I could not see his features, they were shrouded by the drooping felt hat he wore ; but he was tall and splendidly made, and his voice was singularly musical.

'It is here—you are sure of it ?' I heard him say in his rapid French, and with a gesture towards the cottage.

'But, yes,' answered the woman ; 'she

have herself told it me. You can call—ask
—see for yourself.'

'Not possible,' he said as they passed on ;
' she would not help me now.'

'Not help you !' screamed the shrill voice
of his companion. ' *Nom de Dieu!* she would
give you her last farthing. She is fool enough
still.'

Then they passed out of earshot.

I stood there trembling and disturbed. Of
whom had they spoken—of whom could they
have spoken save Nancette ? Yet this evil-
looking woman, this strange man—what had
they in common with my beautiful, ill-fated
girl ? I grew sick at heart with a sudden
dread. I turned away, and went towards the
house. Mid-way between it and the dark
cedar-tree I saw a white figure. It was
Nancette. She came hurriedly towards
me.

' Where are the boys ?' she asked.

I told her I did not know.

'Probably,' I added, 'at M. St. Jean's.'

'Babette has just come in, and told me there was a rumour in the town that a mad dog had broken loose. I hope they are not there.'

'Not likely,' I said cheerfully; 'they are sure to be home directly. I never knew them in later than nine.'

'Let us go to the gates and watch,' she said, and took my arm.

I turned at once. We opened the gate, and went a few yards down the road.

'There they are,' I said, as I caught sight of the two young figures hurrying up the road in the clear, pale moonlight.

'What makes them run so fast?' she said suddenly.

'It is one of their races,' I answered.

But then, even as I spoke, a spasm of fear seemed to catch my heart. No schoolboy racing this; something of fear or terror surely lent wings to those flying feet, and set its

impress upon the white young faces.   Like a
whirlwind they came upon us.

' In—for Heaven's sake, in !' shouted Basil,
and seized my arm.

I was off my feet before I knew anything
more.   Stewart was just on my heels.   The
gate clanged.

' Nancette !' I screamed.   ' Oh, Heaven,
look at her !'

For, like one paralyzed and immovable,
that white figure stood in the centre of the
moonlit road, and rushing straight at her,
with open fangs, and foaming jaws, and
bristling hair, was a huge mastiff.   I shut
my eyes.   I felt sick with sudden horror as I
reeled against the iron bars of the gate.   The
next instant the air seemed rent with shrieks,
and hoarse and terrible sounds.   I looked.   I
saw a lithe young form spring arrow-like
before that motionless figure, and, with
superhuman strength, it seized and closed
with the terrible brute.   Then a crowd of

shouting, rushing figures shut them both from sight.

'Oh, Basil, Basil! He. will be killed!' cried Stewart's voice of agony beside me.

Even as he spoke, a shot rang through the air—clear, sharp, distinct.

The crowd seemed to part and sway aside. In an instant I was among them. I had a confused sense of faces, voices—a stain of blood on the white road—a motionless form outstretched in harmless savagery ; and then —then through them all strode that pale young hero. One arm was hanging down ; a bright crimson stain was on the loose white flannel sleeve.

' Don't touch me,' he said, as Nancette, with a low, faint cry, stretched out her trembling hands. ' It's nothing—only a scratch ; but I'm going to M. St. Jean. He'll put me right—he's got a system of his own for it.'

Then he turned away and ran full speed in the direction of the Frenchman's cottage.

Nancette turned to me.

'He was bitten,' she said; 'he will die!
and for me—for my unworthy sake! Oh,
don't hold me, Myra; let me go to him. It
is all I can do.'

She wrung her hands in desperate misery.
I still held her firmly.

'You can do nothing,' I said. 'But he was
right. If anyone can cure him, it is M. St.
Jean. He was telling me his system the
other day. Stewart,' I went on hurriedly,
'follow him at once—see M. St. Jean. Tell
him I will be there presently—that I remember all he said. We trust to him.'

My voice broke as I looked at the white
agony of the boy's face. He did not speak;
he only drew his cap low down over his eyes
and hurried off.

The crowd were still about us. I heard
voices murmuring confusedly of the bravery
and courage of the boy, but muttering of
ominous results all the same.

' Who killed the dog ?' I asked at last, drawing back from that sickening stream of still flowing blood.

' I, madame—his owner,' said a soft, courteous voice.

Some one came forward from under the dusky boughs, came forward and raised his hat, and stood looking at me and at Nancette in the clear, luminous June night.

She, as she heard the voice, started and looked up, and I saw the blood fade from her cheeks and lips, and leave them gray and ashen as the hues of death.

Her hand clenched convulsively on my arm ; she shuddered in every limb, then grew rigid as stone.

' *You !*' she cried. ' Oh, it is too much— it is too much !'

Then, suddenly, without sound or warning, she fell across the white moonlit road like a dead and stricken thing.

CHAPTER X.

IN a second those strong arms had raised her from the ground.

'Permit me to take her within,' said the musical voice of this stranger.

I had no choice but to obey, so I followed him and his helpless burden. The gates closed behind us—closed on a tragedy that a few brief moments had seen enacted. Sick and trembling with fear for Nancette, for the brave boy—for our whole joint peace and welfare—I crossed the lawn and entered the house.

'Bring her here,' I said, opening the parlour-door.

He obeyed, and laid her gently on the

couch, and stood there silently looking on, as I sprinkled her face with water and loosened the folds of her dress at her throat. She soon opened her eyes and sat up. He withdrew a little into the background as she leant her head against me.

'Myra,' she whispered faintly, 'has he gone, or was it fancy?'

I grew somewhat embarrassed.

'The gentleman,' I said, 'who killed the dog, is here. He brought you home.'

The blood flushed to her face in a burning glow. She rose, and stood there with one hand clasping the loosened lace at her throat, the other steadying her against the couch. He stepped forward. I saw their eyes meet like a flash of challenge and defiance.

'This meeting is a surprise, M. de Volens,' she said coldly. 'I thank you for your service, but I must beg you to excuse me now. The shock, the horror of that terrible scene——'

She shuddered, and grew as white as her dress.

'I have to offer a thousand apologies,' he said, 'for the misfortune of owning that dog. I am deeply distressed at the catastrophe, but your young relative was so impetuous.'

'He saved my life,' she interrupted passionately. 'At what a cost—at what a sacrifice Heaven only knows!'

She clasped her hands before her eyes, as if to shut out the horrors of that scene. I thought it was now my turn to interfere. I looked straight at the cool, watchful, handsome face.

'I am sure you will excuse us,' I said. 'Mrs. Glendenning is very much upset, and I am all anxiety to see after our young hero.'

He bowed low. There was a chill, cruel smile on his lips.

'I am desolated to withdraw,' he said. 'But under the circumstances I feel it is my

duty. The young hero has my deepest com-
miseration.'

Yet I seemed to know, even as if words had
framed it, that in his own cruel heart he was
rejoicing that the boy should suffer now for
the vengeance he had sworn on him at their
last meeting. I seemed to breathe more
freely when that hateful presence had withdrawn itself. I went with Nancette to her
room, and persuaded her to lie down.

'I will tell you all that M. Jean says,' I
said to her again and again. 'You can do
no good by going there. I know he has a
pet theory of his own for treating such cases.
He has spoken of it as infallible. We need
not fear. The boy is in safe hands.'

Gradually she seemed convinced. The
horror of the boy's possible fate seemed
to have obliterated all softer memory of
Pierre de Volens.

At last I left her.

How I reached M. Jean's cottage I hardly

know. It was some half-mile nearer the
town than our own. But, panting and
breathless, I found myself there at last.
Stewart met me in the doorway, his eyes
red and swollen with weeping.

'No one can see him,' he said. 'M.
Jean is going to keep him here for forty
days.'

Then a little dusky figure crept out into
the dark hall.

'It is horrible!' she said. 'But oh, how
brave, how noble of him! How proud I
feel! Do not you?'

I shuddered there in the warm summer
night.

'Is it you, Léonie? Can I see your
father?' I asked.

'Yes; he said he would see you. You
would be calm and sensible. Stewart,' she
added contemptuously, 'does nothing but cry
—as if tears would help one!'

'Is that Madame Freere?' said the voice

of the old Frenchman. 'Will she have the goodness to enter ?'

I entered, sick at heart and trembling. My courage seemed all gone, now that I must hear the doom of that bold and bright young life.

M. Jean led me into a small room like a study, and shut the door.

'Be seated, madame,' he said kindly. 'Why, how white and trembling you look ! I thought all English ladies so brave, so strong. Now do not speak ; I know all you would say. I will do all I can. Everything is in his favour. First, to commence, he was in a profuse heat. Bon ! He is young, healthy, strong. Also good. He have run all the way the moment he was bitten to my house. Still more good. He came here in a great perspiration. Nothing could be better. I have give him the vapour-bath at thirty degrees centigrade. It was strong to suffocating. But we will see—we will see. I keep

him here under my own eye.   I know every
symptom.   It may be forty days or less
before the malady shows of itself.   If not by
then, he is safe.   You need have no more of
fear.'

The tears were rolling down my cheeks as
he finished.   I felt utterly unnerved and un-
strung.   It seemed so horrible to contemplate
that brave young life sacrificed to a fate so
cruel.

'Do you think,' I asked feebly, 'that he
had better remain here, under your own roof?
Won't it inconvenience——'

'Inconvenience!' he burst in indignantly.
'Of what is that?   I like him, I honour
him, I admire him.   It is to my credit and
happiness to save him—and save him I will.
But if he go to you—to crying women, all
fussy, and nervous, and trembling at every
look and movement of the boy, he will be
frightened of himself.   No; he shall see but
me and Léonie.   Léonie is brave; she will

laugh at him. Never will she show fear;
and then, a month—six weeks, and I send
him back to you cured. *Violà !'*

'But,' I said, 'did you not cauterize the
place? I thought that was the safest
plan.'

He shrugged his shoulders with contempt.

'Engleesh,' he said; 'not my method—
not my treatment. It stand to reason the
poison is not in the one place; it go straight
through the blood—everywhere. You cannot burn it out. It must be forced out of
the system. There is no way so effectual as
the *bain vapeur.* I give him that every day
for several days. I keep him here under
mine own eye, quiet, and rational, and composed. Are you agreed?'

'I would agree to anything that would
save him!' I cried passionately. 'Need you
ask?' Then I rose. 'Can I see him?' I
asked timidly.

'No,' was the firm rejoinder; 'it is best

not. You will agitate him. He is best in
his own chamber—quiet.’

‘Was he very badly bitten ?’ I asked again.

‘Not so bad as might have been. It is
the wrist. There will be always a scar. Do
you know—can you describe what sort of
dog ?’

‘A mastiff,’ I said ; ‘a big, ferocious-look-
ing creature.’

Then I stopped, and coloured in confusion.
I could not say the owner was his son, yet I
thought it strange if Pierre de Volens had
come here to the island that he should not be
under his parent’s roof. I saw more compli-
cations arising, our pleasant intercourse
threatened, our friendship at an end, since it
was not possible that Nancette and Pierre
could meet and associate with each other.

‘Ah, a mastiff !’ said M. St. Jean
thoughtfully. ‘That is bad. What wonderful courage ! Sublime—astonishing ! That is
like the English boys—what you call dare-

devil. I know at the school—ah, their tricks, their games, their sports, all dare-devil —all dare-devil! But he saved madame's life, *n'est ce pas?* That was brave—that was fine. Ah, when he go back to school, but how they will regard him—*un vrai* hero! It is true. He will be the king of all the dare-devils there!'

This hopeful view of the case somewhat roused my spirits. I said good-bye to the kindly little man and Léonie, and then left with Stewart. As we went out at the gate, a window was suddenly opened in the room above the porch. I caught a momentary glimpse of a face, then something white flashed out and fell at my feet. I looked, and saw it was a letter addressed to me. It was written in pencil in Basil's large, bold hand. When I reached home I read it.

'DEAR MRS. FREERE,

'Don't worry about me, and don't let Lady Nancye worry either. I'm all right,

and there's nothing to fear; only I must give
in to old Jean's crotchet, or he'll never forgive me.   It was only a scratch after all;
and when I think of *her*, and what it might
have been, I'm as pleased as anything.   I
kept the brute off her.   Do you know who
shot it?   Ask Lady Nancye.   Tell her, if
she loves me, not to have anything to do with
that sneak of a Frenchman again.   She'll
know what I mean.   I suppose I can't come
home for a few days.   I might begin to *bite*.
Love to you all.   Don't be duller than you
can help.

' Yours,

' Basil.'

The note was so characteristic of the boy
that I laughed despite my foolish tears as I
read it; and then, with it in my hand, I went
to Nancette's room.   She was lying down
clad in her loose white wrapper.

Her anxious eyes sought mine with feverish eagerness.

'Good news !' I said cheerfully. 'He is all right. And M. Jean thinks he will remain so. But he is to stay there for the present under treatment.'

She drew a deep breath of relief. The tears came in a swift flood to her eyes.

'My noble boy !' she said ; 'my noble boy ! Oh, I was not worth such a deed.'

'Indeed, you were,' I said, 'and he evidently thinks so. See what he has written. Perhaps the sight of his hand-writing will convince you that he is safe and well.'

She took the note from me and read it eagerly. I saw the colour flush her white cheeks with a sudden vivid glow. She laid the letter down at last, and turned to me.

'What am I to do ?' she said. 'You know who it was? He is here. How can I avoid him ? The same roof that shelters Basil will also shelter him. Oh, Fate is too hard—too hard !'

'You must leave here,' I said; 'there is no other way.'

'But the house — you took it for two months ?'

' True,' I said ; ' but that cannot be helped. We must give it up.'

' And Basil——'

' Basil,' I said, ' is under the care of M. Jean. He must remain there for several weeks. We can do no good by staying.'

She rose suddenly and walked across the room and seated herself by the open window.

' No, Myra—no,' she said. ' He is suffering for my sake. I cannot leave him for my own selfish convenience. This man is nothing to me — nothing. Why'—with a sudden flush and a strange look of passionate resentment, ' do you know he was nearer to me than Basil ; he saw my danger even more clearly, yet he did not move. He—he was afraid. This is the second time Basil has saved me. My gratitude to him outweighs

a hundred times the force of an unworthy
fancy. I will not leave him till I know that
all danger is past.'

For a moment I was silent.

' Do you think,' I said at last, ' that you
have the strength ? Remember to-day.'

' It was not an emotion,' she said, ' so much
as the shock and horror ; the sight of Basil
with that brute's teeth fastened on him, the
streaming blood, the sickening fear of something still more terrible. Ah !' clasping her
shuddering hands over her eyes, ' shall I ever,
to the longest day I live, forget it ?'

' You need not forget it,' I said, ' neither
need you wilfully run into danger.'

' Do you think,' she asked, meeting my
eyes with a quiet surprise in her own, ' that
there is danger—now ?'

' I know,' I said, ' that in an area limited
to thirty miles—is it not thirty miles ?—it
will be difficult to avoid meeting this new and
unwelcome visitor. I know that such meet-

ings must be painful as they are undesirable.
I wish you to understand this fully.   It will
be of no use to come to me when too late,
and say I did not warn you.'

'What do you dread?' she asked, looking
at me quietly and directly, without flush or
tremor now.

'Everything,' I said impulsively.   'I am
afraid of that man—of the woman who was
his companion to-night, of his fatal attrac-
tions, of the possibility of his resuming his
lost power over you, of——'

She stayed me with the light touch of her
hand upon my own.

'You need not be,' she said.   'If there was
any danger—any fascination—I would be the
first to yield to your counsel.   But it has
died out of my heart for ever.   You can't
recall the flame to dead ashes.   That wild,
foolish love is dead, and cold, and gray, as
they would be.   Do you believe me?'

I looked at her long and steadfastly—at

the dark, deep eyes that were so sad and earnest, at the firm chiselled lips—the whole grave, serious meaning of the beautiful young face.

'I believe you,' I said at last; 'but oh, my dear, my dear, there is a base passion in men that pursues the more hotly for coldness, for denial, for the change that has turned love like yours to bitterness! I do not fear you, but *for* you. Pierre de Volens is not a man to be thwarted or baffled with impunity. I could read that in his eyes to-day.'

For an instant her self-command seemed shaken. The pallor of her face deepened, and a cold, gray shadow seemed to rest upon its beauty.

'It would not be so hard for me,' she said, low and regretfully, 'if my husband were by my side. But I drove him thence, and I must fight my battle alone.'

I knelt beside her, and drew her cold hands into mine.

' Do not fight,' I said entreatingly ; ' take my advice, and withdraw. Believe me, it will be wisest—safest—best.'

' Would you have me turn coward ?' she said, with a faint, chill smile. ' How can I tell the worth of my weapons if I do not try them ?   I wish to convince myself that I am cured of my folly ; to retreat would be cowardly.'

I said no more.

CHAPTER XI.

THREE days since I have opened my journal! That shows they have been uneventful—up till to-day.

Basil is still quite well. That is the report as Stewart and I go over every morning to inquire. Sometimes we see his face at the window, less bright and ruddy now by reason of his enforced confinement to the house. Once he opened it and threw out a letter for Nancette. She has not accompanied us yet, for Pierre de Volens is here—under his father's roof, and my worst fears are realized. I have not met him, and Nancette has not been out beyond our own grounds.

To-day, however, as I went down to St.

Peter's Port, I saw him. He was talking to the stout Frenchwoman with whom I had seen him that terrible evening. I began to wonder what they had in common, these two. She did not look like a lady—that I decided quickly in my own mind—yet she seemed on friendly and confidential terms with him.

Stewart was with me, and, as we passed the two, he started visibly.

' Do you see that man ?' he asked quickly. 'He is the same who came over to Owl's Roost, and Mr. Glendenning said he was never to set foot there again. Fancy his being here !'

' Did you not know he owned the dog ?' I asked.

' What, the dog that bit Basil ? No. I've never seen him till now. Basil hates him, I know. Does he know he's here ?'

' Yes,' I said. ' But come, let us hurry on. I don't wish him to see us.'

' I think he has seen us,' said the boy, as

I quickened my steps. 'Yes,' glancing back in the direction of the talkers; 'he has left that lady and is coming after us.'

I said nothing, but walked on at the same pace. We turned out of the badly-paved, irregular main street, and went on towards the sea-wall.

The Esplanade was almost deserted. The hot noonday sun was streaming down on the glittering sea and the picturesque, irregular pile of Castle Cornet. A few fishing-boats lay idly moored in the harbour, and here and there a sail gleamed far out on the quiet waters. Tired and hot with our quick walk, I sat down to rest. Stewart, boy-like, grew impatient of quietude, and wandered off to the edge of the Esplanade to watch the boats.

A minute later a tall figure stood between me and the level sunrays. I knew instinctively whose it was.

'Madame will excuse,' said a voice in

tolerably good English. ' I have the honour
to inquire after the health of her friend. I
trust she is better.'

I bowed stiffly.

' Thank you—yes,' I said. ' She is quite
well now.'

He hesitated a moment, evidently ill at
ease.

' Is madame at liberty to receive visitors ?'
he said at last. ' I have wished to do
myself the honour of calling upon her.
May I venture to do so to-day, as I leave
the island to-morrow ?'

The news was so welcome that I fear my
face must have shown my relief. With an
effort I steadied my voice, and looked up at
him.

Handsome ?—yes, he certainly was handsome, with the type of handsomeness that
wins a girl's beauty-loving eyes. To me his
face was almost repulsive. The brown waves
of hair were not guiltless of the hairdresser's

art ; the smooth, clear skin had faint traces
of bismuth ; the drooping moustache was
carefully waxed and curled ; the long lashes
betrayed a darkening touch that added to
the sombre beauty of the eyes, yet spoke out
the artifice of the toilet here in the pitiless
glare of the searching sunlight.

' Make-up ' in a woman is barely ex-
cusable ; in a man it is revolting.

With a slight gesture of contempt, I drew
away from this artificial Adonis.

' M. de Volens,' I said quickly, ' as the
friend of both Mr. and Mrs. Glendenning, I
must frankly tell you that a visit from you is
both intrusive and undesirable. There is
nothing to warrant a renewal of acquaintance, and Mrs. Glendenning most assuredly
does not wish it.'

He looked at me steadily and unflinch-
ingly.

' You are Mrs. Glendenning's friend ?' he
said with a slight impertinent raising of the

brows. 'Yes ? Very well. But permit me
to say that my business with her is a matter
of serious importance, and admits of no third
person's interference. You will convey my
respects to madame, and say I do myself the honour to call this afternoon.
Yes ?'

'I will do no such thing,' I said indignantly, as I rose from my seat and faced him
there in the glow of sun and sea. 'You
have no right to ask it. I know the whole
sad story of Nancette's past life. I know
how you have been her evil genius—have
spoilt all the fresh fair years of her youth by
your selfish passion. I have her authority
for what I say. She will not see you or
speak to you again.'

I saw his lips grow white beneath the
shade of their thick moustache. He flashed
one quick glance of baffled rage and menace
at me, as, cold and self-possessed, I stood
there before him.

'She has told you—this?' he asked. 'She has commissioned you to say so to me?'

'Yes,' I answered.

For a moment he was silent; then he looked up and met my eyes, a flash of insolent defiance in his own.

'I do not believe you,' he said. 'No; much as I regret being rude to a lady, I do not believe you. In the first place, she could not have told you everything. There is a secret between us which she cannot divulge. It parted her from her husband; it made her marriage but a mockery. Think you I do not know that he—this Englishman who stole her from me—has never lived with her for one single hour since he knew, or fancied he knew, what led to her accepting him. She has not told you that? No; I see it in your face. Well, say this then to her: I claim to see her again by right of our secret. She will not dare to say me nay.'

A strange sick feeling stole over me as I

heard those words, as I read their meaning by light of the cruel secret which had parted Errol from his wife—which had kept her silent even to me on this one point.

I drew myself up with what dignity I could.

'I do not understand you,' I said. 'But I imagined it would not be necessary to tell a gentleman twice that his presence was an unwelcome intrusion.'

He bowed ironically.

'Madame is candour itself,' he said. 'I regret that our interview could not be more agreeable. I shall present myself at madame's charming domicile this afternoon all the same. It will be better that I am received.'

He raised his hat, and passed on, leaving me standing there helpless and be-wildered.

For one swift instant my thoughts turned with an overmastering sense of longing to that absent friend, whose presence was becoming daily more needful.

'Oh, Errol—Errol,' I cried in my heart, 'why don't you come back—why don't you come back!'

I called Stewart, and we turned back from the Esplanade, and took one of the carriages, waiting by the landing-stage, home. I was too tired and too upset by this interview to walk.

The heat was sultry and intense. There was not a breath of air. The roads seemed parched, the very flowers drooped and sickened in the scorching sunlight. There had been no rain or storm since we had come to the island. I glanced up at the brazen skies with a sort of longing for one or other.

'I think there will be a storm before night,' said the driver, as we reached our gates at last.

' I hope so,' I said mechanically, as I paid him his fare ; ' we need it.'

Nancette was just within the gates, watching for us. She wore one of her simple creamy muslins, and held a large white umbrella over her head. I sent Stewart on, and took her arm, and turned aside with her under the trees.

'Something has happened,' she said quickly. ' Basil—is he worse ?'

' No—no,' I said ; ' it is not Basil. Only I have seen——'

' Pierre ?' she cried breathlessly.

I nodded.

' Yes,' I said ; 'he insists upon coming here this afternoon. I told him you would not receive him. He said you must.'

' I *must!*' she faltered. Then setting her small white teeth together : ' I will not !' she cried fiercely. ' Do you hear, Myra—I will not. Nothing shall induce me.'

' I told him that,' I repeated. ' I might

as well have spoken to a stone ! He defied
me to prevent it—he defied you to refuse it.
He is coming.'

'But what can be his reason ?' she cried
desperately. 'There is no use, no sense—
nothing to be gained by forcing himself thus.
What does he require ?'

'That,' I said, 'is more than I can tell
you. He did not favour me with his confidence, but he was very imperative.'

She looked at me helplessly.

'What am I to do ?' she said. 'It is not
that I am afraid, only—only——'

'I know,' I said. 'He has some right
over you, and he uses it unscrupulously.
Your position is an unfortunate one. If
your husband were here he would never dare
behave like this ; but he knows you are un-
protected, alone ; and he is a selfish, unprin-
cipled coward. Oh, Nancette, how could
you, even in the frenzy of romance, ever
have put faith in such a man ?'

She drew her breath sharply.

‘ I am bitterly punished,’ she said—
‘ bitterly. I see my folly now more plainly
every day—every hour that I live.’ Then
she turned to me, her eyes a flame of wrath.
‘ He will drive me desperate !’ she said. ‘ I
cannot bear to be persecuted like this ! It
is brutal, shameful, unseemly !’

‘ It is what he is himself,’ I said. ‘ Ah,
my dear, when we reap our harvests we
regret the seed we have sown.’

She looked at me steadfastly and long.

‘ Myra,’ she said, ‘ I will *not* see him.
You must tell him so. All that is possible
to say between us has been said. For the
rest, I do not see that my husband’s money
should find its way to his pockets any longer.’

‘ Do you mean to say——’ I cried indignantly.

‘ I mean to say,’ she went on, her cheeks
flaming to scarlet, ‘ that it is money he
needs, and money his accomplice needs ; but

they shall have no more. Of that I am determined.'

I took her hand and looked at her.

'Oh, Nancette,' I cried, 'how foolish you have been!'

'Yes,' she said, 'I have. You can't say worse of me than I say of myself. But I will leave this as a written message for him. I will have nothing more to say to him, or to do with him. My mind is made up. I have nothing to fear now.'

'Not—the secret?' I said.

The colour left her face.

'It has done its worst,' she said hopelessly—'it has poisoned my life, and turned my husband's heart from me for ever. Nothing can undo that wrong. If I were a stronger woman,' she added suddenly, as she looked up at the burning width of sky—'if I were not such a weak, cowardly thing—frightened of herself as well as of others—I would have vengeance, not patience!

Heaven knows I have borne enough for this man's sake! He might hold his hand now.'

I was silent. What could I say that would help her, or give her comfort in an hour like this?

She moved away, and I followed her into the house.

A short time afterwards she came to me with a note addressed to Pierre de Volens.

' Will you give him that ?' she said simply. ' I shall go over to Sark this afternoon. You can say I have left here. He will understand.'

I took the note. We then went into the parlour and had our luncheon. I wished her to take Stewart with her, but she refused.

' I am not fit company for anyone,' she said. ' I had rather be by myself.'

Half an hour later, she left the house in a hired carriage for St. Peter's Port. As I kissed her at the door, a strange feeling came over me. I could not analyze or express it, but I felt reluctant to let her go away alone.

'If you would only take Stewart,' I pleaded, as I held her hand, 'I should feel so much more at ease.'

She shook her head.

'No—I am better alone,' she said; 'and the sea is so calm, there is nothing to fear. You will see me back safe and sound this evening.'

'If there is a storm?' I said doubtfully, as I looked up at the burning sky. 'It is so sultry, so oppressive. I am afraid the weather will change.'

'If it does,' she said, 'I can stay in Sark. There is a capital hotel there.'

'I wish I could come with you!' I cried suddenly. 'Could we not leave the note, and both go to Sark?'

'I would rather you saw him,' she said.

'He will read the letter here. I want you
to be present, in case he has anything to
say.'

I did not argue more. Again I kissed the
pale, lovely face, and then watched the
carriage as it took the steep, shady road
down to the town. When I could see it
no more, I turned back into the house. It
was only two o'clock. I wondered how long
I should have to wait. The window was wide
open, but not a breath of air stirred the cur-
tains. The heat was almost suffocating. I
felt oppressed as by a heavy weight. The
silence everywhere was so complete, that the
very rustle of my dress on the matting which
covered the polished floor sounded ominously
loud and irritating. I drew a large easy-
chair up to the window. The outside blinds
were down, and kept off the glare of the sun;
the room was dark, and as cool as it was possible for anything to be on such a day. I
took up some scattered sheets of paper, and

entered all the occurrences of the day ready for my journal.

*   *   *   *   *

I have been writing for nearly two hours. Still Pierre de Volens has not come. Perhaps——

CHAPTER XII.

SEVEN P.M.—The storm has come at last. For three hours has the rain been pouring in torrents from the heavy thunder-clouds that have covered the sultry sky. For three hours have I been in this room, too restless for work, or books, or employment. In despair I sit down to my journal again. I will enter the account of Pierre de Volens's visit. That at least will pass away the time till Nancette returns.

It was but a few minutes after four when Babette ushered him into the little drawing-room, where I sat writing by the window. Coming out of the light into this darkened room, he did not seem to recognise me. He walked up to the little table and bent down to the figure sitting so quietly there.

'Nancette,' he said, in a low, eager voice.

I rose to my feet. I took up her note and held it towards him.

'Mrs. Glendenning has left Guernsey,' I said. 'She desired me to give this note to you. I am sorry you have had the trouble of coming all this way for nothing.'

His face grew very white. Looking at him in that dim light, I acknowledged that he was strikingly handsome. He had made the best of his natural advantages, and the pallor of his face only gave a new charm to the soft darkness of eyes and lashes.

'Left Guernsey!' he said at last. 'It is not possible!'

'It is not only possible, but an accomplished fact,' I said coolly, as I drew the blind up to let some light into the room. 'Her letter explains it.'

He tore it open without ceremony or

apology. At the same moment a low, ominous roll of thunder broke the stillness without. Glancing up, I saw that the sky was dark with looming clouds. A few large drops of rain fell pattering on the leaves of the camellias and geraniums that grew outside the window. I glanced at Pierre de Volens. The note was very brief, but the baffled passion and fury in his heart wrote themselves in ugly living letters across his face as he took in the meaning of its curt lines. He folded it up, and looked straight at me as I stood there by the open window.

'I can guess whom I have to thank for this,' he said, with scarcely-veiled insolence. 'You are a true friend to monsieur the absent husband.'

'I hope,' I said calmly, 'that I should be a true friend to any woman persecuted by a cruel and unmanly man.'

'Meaning—me?'

'Meaning,' I said, 'you—if you have the

sense to take it, monsieur. I warned you
this morning that it would be useless to
attempt to see Mrs. Glendenning again. You
see I was right.'

' I see,' he said ironically, ' a clever woman
who has used her brains against mine to some
advantage. But I am not used to be baffled.
Your advice has simply altered my plans. It
will not be difficult to discover where Madame
Glendenning has fled. The world is never so
small as when one person is trying to hide
from another. We shall meet yet—do not
fear. I can wait—oh yes, I can wait!'

' What do you want with her?' I cried
passionately. ' What is the use of this sense-
less persecution? You have done her harm
enough. Can you not be content?'

He smiled.

' Madame is superb,' he said, ' when she is
a little what we call—*enragée*. But like all
her charming sex, she is not logical. I have
done no harm yet. I do not say what I may

do if put to the test. I have a matter
of business to settle with my fair cousin.
It must be settled. Then I make my
adieux.'

'You want money,' I cried, losing all
patience now. 'You are one of those men
who trade on women's folly and weakness for
your own ignoble ends. Ah!' setting my
teeth firmly in a paroxysm of passionate
indignation, 'if I were only a man! If
for five minutes I could be a man, to chastise
you as you deserve!'

He only smiled, though his lips shook a
little.

'Do not utter a wish that would so punish
the sex you honour by belonging to it,' he
said sarcastically. 'Your tongue can give
chastisement strong enough to please any
man. Be content.'

I was too furious to answer. I watched
him coolly fold up Nancette's letter and put
it in his pocket. Then he walked to the

door. As his hand rested on the handle, he turned his insolent face towards me again.

'You seem to be in your friend's innermost confidence,' he said. 'Pray has she told you with whom she eloped from school before ever M. Glendenning appeared on the scene? If she has, you may allow that I have a little claim on her consideration.'

Then the door closed. I was left standing there like one stunned, trying to fathom the meaning of those insulting words.

Over and over again have I said them to the accompaniment of the falling rain and the crashing thunder. Over and over again have I assured myself they were but the utterance of malice and baffled passion. Yet I only seem to see more clearly the very possibility I deny. I read by light of that cruel taunt all the mystery and misery of Errol Glendenning's marriage.

The secret to which Nancette has alluded —the oft-repeated declaration that the gulf between her husband and herself can never be crossed or closed—the power this man wields over her—all these things startle me with fresh conviction even as I bring against them my own staunch belief in the purity and innate nobility of Nancette's mind.

So the hours have passed—the long, dreary, miserable hours. I am still sitting here alone, while the storm rages without. I am still battling with disbelief, and still listening with longing ears for the sound of the wheels that will tell me of Nancette's return.

8 p.m.—She has not come. The rain still falls, a thick fog is sweeping over the sea, a gray haze of vapour spreads between earth and sky. I begin to hope she may not have left Sark. I know the danger of these Channel fogs. And she is all alone. Oh, with what vain yearnings I long to be beside her !

10 p.m.—Still no signs of her coming.

The storm is over now, but away out to

sea the haze is still thick as ever. I am getting terribly uneasy. I sit here all alone. Babette has gone to bed. So has Stewart. There is not a sound in the house, and that eerie sense of stillness and loneliness which the night brings, is oppressively perceptible.

If she does not come home in another hour, I shall know it is hopeless to expect her. Probably the boat would not run in this fog, and she must be staying in the neighbouring island.

11 p.m.—She has not come. I have grown tired of my own company, and of waiting. I am going to close my journal and betake myself to bed.

CHAPTER XIII.

Is it only a day since I wrote that last extract? A day! It seems to me like years—long, terrible, agonizing years.

Nancette has not returned—nay, more, she has not been to Sark at all. I have exhausted every kind of inquiry—all in vain. The driver says he took her to the harbour, that she paid him, and then went down towards the landing-stage. He drove off, and saw no more of her.

From that moment she seems to have as completely disappeared as if earth or sea had swallowed her. I can find no trace of her going on board the excursion steamer. There is no trace of her at any of the hotels; no boatman appears to have taken any lady out in his boat during the afternoon answering to her description in any particular.

The whole day has passed, and I am well-nigh frantic with my futile efforts. I have called the services of the police to my aid, but the legal arrangements here are so cumbrous and unsatisfactory, that I cannot reckon upon any efficient aid.

So many formalities have to be gone through, that I declare a person might be dead and buried before any steps could be taken to ascertain the fact.

Night has fallen again, and weary and exhausted I sit here trying to surmise and invent theories for her absence, but miserably conscious that my efforts are futile, and that a dread and horror are slowly and surely undermining my attempts at reasonable suggestions.

For Pierre de Volens has left the island also. I learnt that this morning.

As I remember his look, his words, a sort of horror seizes me. I know him to be unscrupulous. I know that he was furious at Nancette's letter, at her absence, which had thwarted his intentions. Supposing they had met !

But no. I shall go mad if I pursue that train of thought !

It is nearly midnight now. I cannot rest, I cannot sleep. The police officers have promised to let me know the moment any news is ascertained. At any moment some message might come, and I must wait and hope for it.

I think of her to-night as I never thought of her before—I tell myself it is impossible she could have deceived me. Surely— surely Pierre de Volens has lost his power over her. Surely not even the dastardly insinuations of his last words to me could form the basis for such an inexplicable thing as

Nancette's flight—as Nancette's disappearance.

The dawn is breaking in the east—the clear,
pale, lovely dawn of a summer day. I see
the rose-tints of the sky reflected in the sea.
I watch the mists as they furl themselves in
hazy vapour, and float mysteriously into the
mystic clouds.

Another day! What will it bring? What
fate has befallen the young, sorrowful, tragic
life that has become so dear to me?

I look down the familiar garden-path. I
seem to see her as she stood there yesterday — the simple white dress falling in
its graceful lines around the slender figure;
the beautiful, wistful face upraised to
mine beneath the burning haze of sunlight.

A tear falls on the page. My heart calls
for her as never it has called before.

The sun is mellow and golden in the soft

blue above. I hear the stir of the waking birds in the boughs without. All things external are so bright and fair, that they seem a mockery to me in my grief and ever-deepening fear.

In despair I turn away. The shudder of an inexpressible dread shakes me as with icy cold. I think of her in her weariness and sorrow and despair; I think of her wasted life and wasted love, and the relentless perse-cution which had cursed even this brief spell of peace.

Had she been tempted beyond her strength, or tried beyond endurance ? Had the sea claimed her secret for its own, and was the tired heart at rest under those stormy waters ?

If I only knew—oh, dear Heaven, if I only knew !

I take up my narrative a week later.

Nothing has been ascertained of Nancette's

fate. It is as great a mystery as ever. Not all the services of procureur, and deputies, and officials have been of the slightest use. Considering that neither bailiff nor *jurats*, nor even the impressive body called the Elective States, has had the benefit of legal education, this is not so surprising as it might appear at first.

I am utterly disheartened and hopeless now.

The favourite theory here seems to be that the missing girl employed a cutter to take her to one of the adjacent islands, and that the boat must have been lost in the fog, or run into one of the numerous rocks that make the channels of approach so dangerous. Another theory is also advanced that she may have employed one belonging to a boatman of the other islands waiting for a return passenger, or the property of some of the natives who had come over to work at the *vraic* harvest, which had recently commenced, and would be in full swing until August.

I myself have been over to Sark, and Herm, and Alderney, but no trace or sign of her presence is to be found at any of these places.

Sorrowfully but surely does conviction come upon me that her fate is doomed to be unknown. All that is possible to do I have done. Inquiries, agents, money, have produced no result. From the hour that she went down the harbour road to the sea her fate is involved in impenetrable mystery.

At last, sorrowfully and heart-brokenly, I write to Errol. I tell him that he may come back now if he chooses, for never again in all human probability will he see the face of the ill-fated girl who has borne his name, and lived in his home, and cast the shadow of her tragic life upon his heart and my memory.

August 30*th.*—In tears and grief I write these last records.

To-morrow I leave Guernsey with the boys and M. St. Jean. Basil is quite cured ; not a single bad symptom has shown itself. But his grief for the fate of Nancette has made him very ill. I could not have believed that he would have taken it so to heart. We did not tell him until M. Jean gave us leave. He thinks that school-life and English air will subdue the boy's sorrow in some degree, so we are hastening back to Owl's Roost. A very sad and dismal party we are.

Léonie is coming to see us off. In her brusque, cold way I think she is sorry for our sorrow, but she does not say much. I have begun to regard her with a certain distaste. She reminds me of that hateful memory. I have ascertained that Pierre de Volens is in Paris, and alone. I feel ashamed of the unworthy suspicion of a moment, but even as I know it is for ever set at rest, I

feel the shadow of that sad and inexplicable
fate falling darkly, ominously over my heart,
and I close the pages that tell of it, in silence
and in tears.

BOOK IV.

SUSPENSE.

CHAPTER I.

It was the dusk of a cold autumn day. The last rays of sunset were faintly shining through misty clouds ; the trees were showering damp and faded leaves upon the ground ; the quiet of the lonely woods was shadowed and subdued by the melancholy influence of the dying year.

A man was making his way over the leaf-strewn path which led to the gates of Owl's Roost. He trod it as one familiar and acquainted with every landmark. His step was somewhat hurried ; he scarcely glanced around. He walked on steadily as one with an object in view, and only stopped when the tall iron gates that opened on the winding drive arrested his progress.

Passing through them, with a word of explanation to the woman at the lodge, he went on towards the house. The wind rustled the boughs of the trees in the avenue, and the leaves fell damp and cold about his face, and fluttered to his feet. Everything around and about him was dreary, and chill, and inexpressibly gloomy.

The old house was so thickly shut in by trees that it was scarcely visible. Only a few lights gleamed from the windows, and served still further to show up the gloom that shrouded it like a shrouding curtain.

As the stranger advanced and rang the bell, he shuddered from head to foot. The pain of remembered pain turned him cold and faint. He was thinking of a past, bitter with more than the ordinary bitterness of life. He was thinking of one vague dream that had illumined it briefly, only to shroud it in deeper darkness for that momentary light. He was thinking of efforts made

to balance and sustain that life amidst unreasoning passion and cruel pain. He was
thinking of isolated years of youth and man-
hood, and of drifting fancies that had faded
into dim shadows now.

Under the influence of such feelings and
such memories, he found that the door was
open, and that he was confronted by a strange
face.

'I wish,' he said, 'to see Mrs. Freere.'

The woman looked at him as one looks
at a stranger. Then she led the way into
the hall, and across it to a small room cur-
tained off from the library.

A bright fire burned there ; a lamp was on
the table. By the fire a woman sat in a low
cushioned chair.

She started as the door opened, then rose
to her feet with a low, astonished cry.

' Errol !' she cried. ' You ! Is it possible ?'

The soft folds of her black dress fell round
her tall, beautiful figure. The light shone

on her flushed cheeks, and the radiant glow
of welcome in her eyes. She looked a
beautiful woman still, though the first bloom
of youth had passed. The dark background
of rich colours in the room framed her face
and figure to wonderful advantage, and as
she clasped his hands in eager welcome,
Errol Glendenning seemed to recognise for
the first time how fair a woman this friend
of his youth was.

For a moment both were silent ; then
their hands parted. The colour left Myra
Freere's face ; she sank down into the low
chair, and took up a small hand-screen, as
if to shade her face from the glow of the
flames.

'You know all ?' she said, her voice low,
and pained, and unsteady. 'You had my
letters ?'

'Yes,' he said. 'I was very shocked and
—and grieved. Has nothing more been
heard ?'

'Nothing. I do not wish to reproach you, Errol, but I feel more and more every day that if you had only listened—if you had only come back—this would not have happened.'

He had drawn up another chair and sat down opposite her. He leant his arms on his knees and bent his head down on his hands. She saw that his hair had become quite grey. The dejection and misery of his attitude went to her heart.

'I know you have suffered,' she said.

His hands fell. He looked at her with such agony in his face and eyes as stayed the words on her lips.

'*Suffered!*' he said. 'I think no one but myself can realize how much.'

The deep eyes, the worn, haggard features, the loose, thick waves of iron-grey hair, all told a tale that no woman's eyes could read unmoved. There was pity that almost touched the borderland of anguish in hers, as she read the history of that altered face.

'I am not so hard as you have thought me,' he went on, his voice less firm and even now. 'If I had loved her less I might have forgiven more easily, but the wrong was one beyond my strength to bear. I could not forego my own self-respect, even for the sake of that love.'

'Are you sure,' she asked earnestly, 'that there has been no mistake? Mind—I have seen so much of her—I have studied her nature so closely, I could stake my life upon her innocence and truth.'

He shook his head.

'Did she ever tell you,' he said slowly, 'why we parted?'

'No,' said Myra Freere gravely; 'but she always blamed herself.'

He looked away into the blazing fire.

'I thought the story would never cross my lips,' he said; 'but you judge me so

harshly that I feel I owe myself the right
of vindication. Do you suppose that, loving
her as I did, I would have voluntarily
banished myself from her presence had there
not been a compulsory reason for doing so ?
You know me well enough to be sure of
that. Myra, the truth is this : When the
Count de Forèze left me in London, it was
to go to the school where his daughter
lived. For a week after our arrival I saw
and heard nothing of him. At the end of
that time he appeared, changed as if by
years of sorrow and trouble. The secret of
that week I only learnt after Nancette had
become—my wife.'

He paused. The face opposite to him had
become very pale. The hand that held the
screen trembled so, that she laid it on her
lap and let the fire-flames dye her face as
they would.

' When the Count went to the school,' resumed Errol Glendenning, 'he learnt that his

daughter was there no longer. Nor could any trace of her be discovered. She had fled one night, taking a few necessary articles of clothing with her. For a week he sought her like one distraught. At the end of that time he discovered her by means of a newspaper advertisement. She had left the school, and fled with Pierre de Volens. She had remained under the same roof with him, at the house of a Frenchwoman who kept a low boarding-establishment, for that week. The large sum offered by her father for news of her tempted the woman to reveal her whereabouts, and her father came there and took her back instantly. The scoundrel who had decoyed her thence, fled at the first announcement of discovery, and opened negotiations with the father for her hand—and fortune— from a safe distance. The Count swore that he should have no fortune, so intense was his hatred of this man. Thereupon M. de Volens took himself off, leaving the field to me—poor miserable dupe. I heard nothing of the story, but the Count never concealed his intense anxiety that I should become his daughter's husband. The rest of the circumstances—his sudden death, Nancette's forlorn condition, our hurried marriage, all this you know. But if you can fancy my horror at this discovery—if you can picture what I, in the first flush and fervour of my realized love-dream, experienced, first by the appearance of Pierre de Volens, then later on by the discovery of that advertisement from the Frenchwoman telling the Count of his daughter's whereabouts during that week I had deemed her safe and innocent under his protection, if you can fancy this—only you cannot, no woman could—you might be able to fathom in some degree the depths of misery and degradation I sounded on that awful night. Heaven alone preserved my reason and my life. Truly they both looked value-less enough then. At first I thought I could

not endure to live, could not drag this burden
of shame about with me for all the years to
come.   I went away to London.   I think I
was ill for a long time.   I could not think
clearly.   I could not tell what course was
best to take ; but I knew that I could never
live under the same roof with the woman who
had so cruelly betrayed me, who had taken
my name and honour into her unworthy
keeping, and left me bankrupt in love,
and faith, and peace, and home, for all
time.

'When I grew better and calmer I came here
once more.   I thought matters must be put
on some footing between us.   The very day
I came in my shame and agony to the home
her presence had cursed, she was with her
lover on the cliffs yonder.   She had met him
again, and of her own free will.   Then I
seemed to turn to stone.   My love for her
grew bitter as hate, bitter as my scorn for
my own weakness.   There seemed but one

thing to do. The law could not part us unless I offered it a plea. Her fortune was in
my keeping, just as my name and honour
were in hers. I agreed to leave her. I
thought that three years of absence would
plead a just cause for separation, and that in
due course these terrible fetters might be
broken from off my hands and hers. That
was why your letter did not move me, powerful as its pleading was ; that was why
between your picture of her loveliness and
innocence crept always the black cloud of
treachery and shame ; that was why I had
neither will nor power to address her by any
word or in any form ; that was why my
home and country grew hateful in my sight,
and I sought travel, danger, excitement,
death, in any land or place that offered them.
Now,' and he drew a deep breath, and rested
his throbbing temples on his hand—' now,
Myra, you have heard the whole shameful,
pitiful story, you can judge for yourself as to

who deserves most blame, or most compassion.'

If any alloy of baser feelings had mingled
with the pure gold of Myra Freere's noble
and generous nature, she would have been less
worthy to be the friend of the broken and
heart-weary man who had given her his confidence at last.

That no such feeling did enter it, that no
throb of leaping pulse seemed to quicken into
life a long-dead dream that had once vivified
her lonely girlhood, were only surer proof of
the innate loyalty and sterling truth of her
character.

She met his eyes steadily, but with infinite
compassion.

' I do not blame you—now,' she said softly ;
' then I did, most bitterly.   But, despite your
story, I cannot feel convinced of Nancette's
guilt.   She was so young ; she could so
easily have been deceived ; she might, as you
say, have fled to this Frenchwoman's house

thinking her a friend who would protect her, or give her shelter till the necessary formalities for her marriage had been arranged. Then came her father's discovery, his refusal to sanction that marriage or give her the fortune on which Pierre de Volens had so surely counted. Think of her bewilderment, her horror, of disappointed love and faith, of the claims of duty, the shame that her father's interpretation of her conduct brought into her life, and chained to her future as a loathed and hateful secret. Think of all this, and ask yourself if she was after all not more to be pitied than blamed—if her sufferings have not more than atoned for the error that you call sin.'

Errol Glendenning dropped his hand, and raised his worn and haggard face.

'Do you mean to say,' he said in a hoarse, unsteady voice, 'that you think I have misjudged her—that she is not guilty——'

'I mean to say,' interposed Myra Freere,

'that I have lived for nearly two years under the same roof that has sheltered her ; that I have been daily—almost hourly in her companionship ; that I have studied her, watched her, tested her ; that I have heard such portion of her story as she could confide, and now added to it is the sequel of your own—I mean to say that with all this, I believe her to have been infatuated by a foolish fancy— misled, thoughtless, imprudent ; but, despite all, she is innocent as you in your man's reasoning have never believed her to be, since you made that fatal discovery.'

He started to his feet then—amazed, perplexed beyond the expression of mere words. To and fro he paced the room in stormy and defiant silence. She watched him, strong still in purpose and intent—all the stronger because of some faint woman's weakness that whispered at her heart—all the stronger because it would have been so easy to take that other view, to yield up the very defiance

that cost her such bitter pangs—to say
to him :

'You are right : any man would have
acted as you have done, for only a woman,
clear-sighted, generous, self-convinced, and
unreasoning, could read between the narrow
lines that separate a girl's mistake from a
conscious sin—could believe in the reckless-
ness of a romantic folly that yet held no guilty
secret in the background of its foolishness.'

Only a woman—and such a woman as
Myra Freere.

But she did not say this. She only watched
him in silence until at last he came and stood
before her again.

His deep, sad eyes looked back to hers
with a look they had not worn yet—in a
woman's eyes it would have meant the relief
of tears, yet they were dry enough, despite
the trembling of the faltering voice.

'Myra,' he said, 'I have always thought
you the noblest woman that ever breathed;

but till to-night I think I never guessed what
possibilities of nobility remained for me to
discover. I thought all women were ready
to cast a stone at an erring sister; but you
—you are trying to bring back some of my
lost faith—to break up this hard and bitter
crust that has lain between my heart and all
other hearts since that folly cursed my life.
I wish—well, friend as you are I can't tell
you how I wish, that I could share your
belief; but I can't. I seem to have lost all
possibility of trust in her.'

'And yet,' said Myra gravely, 'you loved
her. Is it love to doubt so easily—to give
such grudging faith to the better things in a
woman's nature—such ready credulity to the
worst?'

'It is a man's love,' he said. 'Men form
their ideal—they place it on high in a temple
of purity. Better death than that it should
be defaced, defamed, dragged through the
mire of shame, defiled by evil tongues—the

sport of base and unscrupulous passions! I had placed her so high above all others——'

'That,' said the grave, gentle voice, 'is so foolish. Are you not more to blame for the perfections you imagined, than she for falling short of them?'

He shook his head.

'We argue,' he said, 'from a totally different standpoint. But there is no need of argument at all, her folly is expiated now. Heaven forgive me if in any way I have misjudged her, and Heaven rest her soul!'

The solemn words fell across the stillness of the room like a prayer beside a death-bed —the requiem of an ended life.

The woman sitting there in the glow of the waning firelight bent her head upon her clasped hands in a sudden paroxysm of grief.

'I have done my best,' she said, and a faint sob broke from her and frightened her with its threatened loss of self-command.

'You have been the truest friend that ever man or woman had,' he answered with grave tenderness.

'And yet—' she sobbed brokenly, 'you will not believe !'

For an instant there was dead silence. She looked up and met his eyes, then shrank back startled and appalled by the tale they told.

He folded his arms on the mantel-shelf, and dropped his head on them.

'Heaven help me,' he said, ' I *cannot !*'

CHAPTER II.

THE autumn night had sighed itself away in faint gusts of wind and rain.

It was morning once more—a morning of sunshine and clear sky, and fresh, sweet scents of the late autumn flowers that still held their own against the breath of coming winter; morning, and Errol Glendenning and Myra Freere stood in the library at Owl's Roost indulging in a somewhat stormy dialogue.

'I can't bear to think of banishing you in this unceremonious fashion,' he was saying; 'and to that dreary hole at this most dreary season. At least stay here till I return from Guernsey.'

She shook her head.

'You know of old,' she said, 'I am very determined. I must not offend the awful Mrs. Grundy, even to please you. Besides, you have been banished too long already, and my old roost has been deserted nearly as long. No, Errol, don't waste time in arguments. I leave here this morning, whether you stay or not.'

He looked moodily into the glowing flames.

' I suppose you are right,' he said ; 'a man like myself can't even have a friend.'

' I think,' she said gently, 'you know I shall always be *that*. I simply return to my old home, now that you have no further need of me.'

' You have been very good,' he said—'too good. When I asked that service of you I did not think how much it would cost you.'

She might have said with truth that he

would never know its cost; but she had learnt to school herself too well for any rash admission—for any betrayal of a secret guarded through long and patient years. She only smiled brightly and bravely into his face.

'I have never complained,' she said. 'Indeed, I was most happy and content until—until this awful catastrophe.'

'I do not suppose,' he said, 'that I can learn anything, or do anything more than you, my kind friend, have done. But it will be a satisfaction. I mean to engage a clever detective in Paris, and get him to work out the mystery. If she went out on the sea that day, someone must have taken her, or seen her. I shall have every one of the neighbouring islands scoured and searched —I shall not rest until my own belief is verified.'

'And that belief?' questioned Myra Freere timidly.

'Can you doubt it? She must have perished on that night in the storm.'

'She could swim beautifully,' said Myra, as if hazarding a new suggestion.

'No doubt; but think of those stormy Channel waters—they would tax the endurance of the strongest swimmer, and she was only a delicate, fragile girl.'

'It is sad—terribly sad, to think of such a death,' said Myra Freere with a shudder. 'I can't realise it—can't believe it, even now. Yet, if she had been saved, she must have made some sign—sent some word.'

'Do you cling to such a hope?' he asked drearily. 'I never did from the first.'

He thought of her last words to him on that last day when they had parted:

'*I do not want to live ; I am so unhappy. If I could only die young as my mother did!*'

'She has had her wish,' he said sadly— 'she has had her wish!'

· 'What was that?' asked Myra. 'Surely not—death? She was so young, so fair, so gifted; and, latterly, she seemed so much happier——'

'Until,' he added bitterly, 'that scoundrel crossed her path again.'

'But she had ceased to care for him,' Myra said eagerly. 'Indeed—indeed, she had. She had begun to see him in his true colours—to read the selfishness and brutality of his character aright. I think her foolish infatuation had turned to loathing and contempt; nothing could induce her to see him. The dread and horror of doing so were the cause of her sad fate, if—if it be as we fear.'

For a moment there was dead silence. Then, suddenly, Errol Glendenning seized her hands, and looked searchingly down into her eyes.

'Myra,' he said hoarsely, 'for Heaven's sake, answer me truly from your own brave, honest soul! Are you sure—sure in your

own mind, by light of all you have known
and seen, that she did not act like this to
throw suspicion off her real motives—that *he*
was not concerned in her flight ?'

She wrenched her hands from his, and
faced him with such scorn and anger that
he half recoiled, and for one brief moment
felt as ashamed of his suspicion as she was of
its suggestion.

'No !' she cried passionately—' ten thousand times no ! He had nothing whatever
to do with it. I am sure of it as that I live.
Oh, Errol, shame on you to mistrust her so !
Will you never believe—never ?'

'A faith once broken is hard to mend,' he
said. 'Think of these bitter years.'

'I have thought of them—more often than
you perhaps imagine,' she said. 'But surely
you can believe in what I say ?'

'I believe you have convinced yourself,'
he said. 'But I am made of sterner stuff,
and this blow seemed to turn me into

iron. I was not a hard or suspicious man before.'

'No,' she said quietly; 'you were not. Nor need you be now.'

He turned away and paced the room restlessly. The feverish, bitter aching of his heart stifled all softer pleading. Yet he knew he loved that lost girl still—that every memory of her that had burned into his soul with its cruel pain had yet been powerless to change that feeling. The more he denied its existence, the more passionately it defied his denial. But he was too proud to betray that weakness. He guarded his secret too well for even Myra Freere's keen eyes to read it.

'Do not let us speak of this more,' he said at last. 'Our time is very brief. If—if I am not back by Christmas, will you entertain the boys here for me? I promise you not to intrude. I will scrupulously respect Mrs. Grundy for the future.'

The beautiful face had grown somewhat pale.

‘ Yes,’ she said ; ‘ I will do that gladly. But you will go and see them before you leave ? You will tell Basil your errand ?’

‘ Is he still so devoted ?’ he asked almost bitterly.

‘ Indeed he is. I never saw such fidelity. He has never been the same since her loss. It seemed so hard after his heroism, his sufferings, after that noble deed, never even to see her face, to hear her thanks. I was quite alarmed about him once.

‘ He is young,’ said Errol Glendenning coldly. ‘ The young soon forget. He has not yet learnt the lessons of life.’

‘ He has learnt one lesson,’ she answered— ‘ the lesson of a chivalrous faith. I do not think he will ever forget that ; and now I must leave you. I have my morning visit to pay to poor old Clitheroe. He always looks for it.’

'Deborah has told me what a ministering angel you have been,' he said gently. 'But as I told you long ago, I think you are one of the few good women the world holds.'

How those words echoed in her heart as she sat by the side of the bedridden old man! How they set her pulses leaping as to the music of remembered praise! How, still echoing and thrilling her with sweet content, they followed her from the gloomy house with all its tragedy of bitter love and broken faith, and made her glad and trustful as few words could have had power to do!

But how should he know that, being blind, and self-absorbed, and having lived the best years of his life in ignorance of a treasure that needed but the outstretching of his hand to grasp? How should he know it, noting only the calm friendliness of past days in the frank, sweet eyes that had learned only too well to guard a woman's secret?

So they parted in the cold, faint autumn
sunlight, and the chill of loneliness and
desolation closed once more over the
deserted rooms and empty corridors of Owl's
Roost.

CHAPTER III.

OCTOBER rains were holding their sway over the Channel archipelago. Chill north-east winds sobbed among the poplar-trees and oaks of Guernsey. Fields and copses were shrouded in damp mists; the faint, sickly smell of decaying flowers and leaves reigned everywhere in place of the summer odours of roses and heliotropes, and lilies, and magnolia-blossoms.

Among the rugged cliffs the petrel, and cormorant, and gull circled, and screamed, and fought for their finny prey. The sea was rough and stormy—a mass of frothy currents and dashing waves. It seemed all inexpressibly dreary and mournful to Errol

Glendenning as, after a rough and stormy passage from the French coast, he found himself at last safe at the Guernsey Hotel.

He was accompanied by a short, dark, quiet-looking man, who had been recommended to him by one of the chief *commissaires* of police in Paris as a very able and useful agent for those researches he had come to make.

As their stay in the island was likely to be uncertain in duration, Errol Glendenning made arrangements with the landlord of the hotel to board them by the week. It was a bad time of the year for his researches, but he felt that anything was better than remaining at Owl's Roost with this horrible uncertainty hanging over his head. He had determined to convince himself by searching inquiry and thorough investigation whether a loophole of escape had been possible for Nancette; whether she might not have been picked up by some stray boat, and be all this while on one of the adjacent islands. There were several, he knew, between Alderney and the Casquet rocks that were almost unapproachable and almost uninhabited. Some were supposed to be quite so.

Until he had searched these, as well as the Minquiers and the Douvres, he felt he should never be at rest.

The detective shook his head as they sat together in their private sitting-room that night, and Errol Glendenning produced maps and charts, and explained his plans.

'It will take you months,' he said. 'And at this time of the year it is almost impossible to do anything by way of sea.'

'I am going to charter a steamer,' said Glendenning quietly; 'a stout, strong, seaworthy boat. I will then be able to make use of every glimpse of fine weather we get, and be independent of wind and tide.'

'Ah,' said Paul Lihou, 'that sounds very well; but I have been here before, you

know ; all my boyhood was spent in these
islands. No steamer can be independent of
shoals, and rocks, and reefs on this dangerous
coast. There is a line of sixty miles of them
from Granville to the Douvres. On the side
of the French coast they are impassable,
except for very small vessels. I know them
well. I was for ever on the water when I
was young. I could swim and dive like a
fish. The sea had no perils for me. Once I
took my boat out too far. A sea-fog came
on, and I was for a night and a day on one
of those islands. There was only a fisherman's hut there. It was all rocks and caves.
Not a soul was there ; the owner of the hut
only came over for the *vraic** season. I
lived on sea-birds' eggs and mosses. By
good fortune I had water and bread with me
in my boat. I shall not easily forget that
adventure. When I heard at the Bureau of

* A seaweed found in large quantities in Jersey and
Guernsey. It is chiefly used for manure.

what you desired, monsieur, I said, " I am
the man. I know every foot of that coast.
I have explored places that no other human
being has explored. If any trace can be
found, I will find it." But I tell you it will
be perilous ; it will cost much; it will be
long ; and it will be disheartening.'

'For that I do not care,' said the Englishman calmly. 'My time is my own. Peril
has only a charm for me. Money is no
object, and I am too used to disappointments
to be heartbroken by one more. I would
sooner spend all my life in this search than
remain in uncertainty as to my wife's fate.'

The detective looked keenly at the grave
and weary face.

' He is anxious,' he said to himself; ' but
is it that he loved her so dearly, or that he
wishes to assure himself that he may replace
her without fear ? The minds of these
English are hard to read.'

For a week the weather rendered all sea

expeditions impracticable. Paul Lihou did
not waste time, however. He inquired into
the manner of investigation of the law
dignitaries of Guernsey, and listened to their
accounts of ' superhuman exertion ' with
scarcely-veiled contempt. Accustomed as he
was to the marvellous routine, the un-
exampled proficiency, and tireless energy and
skill of the French police system, his opinion
of the legal constitution of the Royal Courts
was not a very flattering one, but he kept it to
himself in this early stage of investigation,
and used its officials as tools for his own
work, which already he knew would demand
all the coolness and acumen of a trained and
critical mind.

At the end of the week he had learnt no
more than Errol Glendenning already knew,
but he had discovered that there had been
several strange boatmen and fishermen about at
the time of Nancette's disappearance, many of
whom came to be employed in the second

vraic cutting, which lasts from June to August. It was therefore just possible that the missing girl might have taken one of their cutters and gone off to Sark or Herm, or even to one of the less known islands. Certainly it seemed an irrational proceeding, but as the Frenchman said with a shrug of disdain : 'If one begins to question the reasons for a woman's actions, where would one arrive ?'

He had as yet only arrived at a conjecture, and was about to work it out. The result might be nothing, also it might be something. Errol Glendenning was willing to run the risk of improbability leading to a specific result, and accordingly the next proceeding in the plan of campaign was to search the neighbouring islands. The steamer had been chartered, and was at their disposal, and the moment the weather improved they commenced their researches. Glendenning's plan was to go to each island, visit the various

hotels and inns, interrogate the officials at
the landing-place, the owners of boats or
fishing-smacks, or any small vessel that
might have been plying to and fro between
Guernsey and the neighbouring islets during
the summer months. This, as Lihou said,
was a work of time.

If it had not been for the Frenchman's
assistance Glendenning would never have
been able to penetrate the innumerable
caverns, hollows, cliffs, nooks, and headlands
which abound in Alderney, Herm, Sark, and
the Chaussey Islands. It was close on
Christmas time when he resolved to investi-
gate these last. The search was as yet
hopeless and without result.

Before proceeding to the Grande Iles,
Glendenning ran over to Guernsey for letters
and provisions.

At the hotel he found several letters,
awaiting him. One was from Basil—the
first he had addressed to his guardian for

months. The boy briefly stated that he
intended to accompany M. St. Jean and
spend his Christmas vacation in Guernsey
unless he heard from his guardian objecting
to such a proceeding. His object, he said,
was to assist in the search for Nancette or
definite news of her fate that Errol Glendenning was prosecuting. The letter was brief,
earnest, almost tragic in its suppression of
grief, yet plainly betraying how faithfully the
boy's heart clung to its youthful idol. As
Errol Glendenning glanced at the date he
saw that in all probability Basil must have
taken silence for consent and be here already.

He therefore sent a messenger to M. St.
Jean's cottage to ascertain the fact, and, if
Basil should be there, to desire him to come
round to the hotel.

About an hour afterwards the boy arrived.

At the first glance his guardian started.
He saw before him a tall, handsome youth
changed almost out of all likeness to the

wild schoolboy he remembered. But a strange look of suffering and repression had come over the once frank, unclouded face.

They shook hands silently. Both pair of eyes met with a sort of veiled challenge. The boy's chivalrous heart was still resentful of the man's coldness and neglect towards the beautiful, forlorn creature he adored. He felt more ill-disposed than friendly towards him.

' How long have you been here ?' asked his guardian.

' I arrived last night,' answered the boy. ' As you did not answer, I thought you would not object to my coming here.'

' No,' said Errol Glendenning ; ' I do not object. I have heard of your devotion to— to this poor lost girl. I am sorry I have learnt nothing yet as to her fate. My long investigation will soon be at an end. If she were alive—if any accident had detained her all these months in helplessness, I must have discovered it. But her fate seems shrouded in mystery.'

'Will you let me help you—accompany you?' asked the boy eagerly. 'Oh, sir, I shall be so grateful if you will.'

'You are quite welcome to come with me on the steamer,' said his guardian. 'But I understood you were on a visit to your master. It will scarcely be polite.'

The frank young face clouded.

'I think,' he said, 'that M. St. Jean would willingly excuse me. He knows how anxious I was to come here—and for what reason.'

'We both owe M. St. Jean a debt of gratitude for saving your life,' said Errol Glendenning. 'I will call there to-morrow and offer my thanks in person, and also explain your anxiety to accompany me. I am going to the Chaussey Islands now. I should like to start early to-morrow, so

you had best go back to M. St. Jean and tell
him I shall pay him an early visit.'

The boy took up his hat, and, after a few
more questions and explanations, he left the
room.

Errol Glendenning paced to and fro, his
brow moody and clouded. What would he
not have given to hold the simple faith and
trust that this young, chivalrous nature held
—to feel that, despite appearances, prejudices,
mistakes, he might yet love and adore that
beautiful and ill-fated memory! But he
knew that mistrust had eaten into his better
nature, and that, he could not accept
this girl's history as her chivalrous young
knight, and her staunch and loyal friend
had accepted it.

In the midst of these reflections, a knock at
the door aroused him. It opened to admit
Lihou. Errol Glendenning's first glance at the
man's face showed him that something had
happened.

He stopped in his restless pacing. His heart seemed to stand still as with some sudden shock.

'You have learnt something?' he said hoarsely, and he leant his hand on the table as if to steady himself.

'Yes,' said Paul Lihou, 'I have learnt—something. It is not anything like what we expected or supposed. We have been on a false track all along. In the first place, monsieur, you have not been quite open with me. You did not tell me that madame had a lover.'

Glendenning started; the red blood flushed to his brow.

'I—I do not understand you,' he said.

'I will explain,' said the man calmly.

He drew a chair to the table, and sat down.

'I have made acquaintance to-day,' he said, 'with a lady staying at Guernsey for the good of her health. At least, she says

it is for the good of her health. The lady
has heard that an eccentric Englishman has
chartered a steamer here, and spends his
time cruising about, seeking for a missing
wife, popularly supposed to have been
drowned during the summer that is past.
Monsieur will excuse my bluntly stating
facts, for time presses. A steamer leaves
to-night for St. Malo, and I wish monsieur
to accompany me on a little excursion
there.'

'To St. Malo!' faltered Glendenning.

He had grown very pale. He turned
aside, and drew up a chair to the table,
facing that of the detective.

'Tell me all,' he said curtly.

'The lady,' resumed the detective, 'is by
name Madame Lamontaine. Ah,' as Glendenning started, 'monsieur is aware of her.
She said as much. Madame Lamontaine
was in St. Helier's a brief time in the
summer, when the lamented catastrophe took

place. She was leaving by the night-boat for St. Malo, when two passengers hailed the steamer from one of the small islands *en route*. They had taken refuge there from the storm. They were taken on board, and went to St. Malo—Hotel de Creux. The description of the lady is in all respects that of madame for whom we search. The gentleman was dark, tall, singularly handsome——'

'For Heaven's sake,' cried Errol Glendenning, hoarsely, 'stop! I know the rest.'

'I think,' said the detective quietly, as he shut up his notebook, 'we can verify the rest at St. Malo. If the landlord's description tallies with that of the lady from St. Heliers the affair ceases to be mysterious—in effect, it is simply an *affaire d'honneur*, which monsieur must pursue as he pleases. I regret that so much time and money have been wasted. Had monsieur been frank with me from the first——'

‘Stop !’ cried the tortured man. ‘Spare
me any remarks. I—I never thought—
never dreamt of this !’

The Frenchman rose. Hardened as he
was to terrible revelations, to domestic
tragedies, to crimes of all descriptions, he yet
felt a strange compassion for this grave,
self-contained Englishman who suffered so
terribly at .the hands of a woman, and that
woman his wife.

‘I deplore monsieur’s sufferings,’ he said
gently ; ‘though he is not the first by many
who has learnt, through me, of what a
woman’s treachery is capable. Is it monsieur’s wish to accompany me to St. Malo ?’

‘Yes,’ said Glendenning, after a brief
hesitation ; ‘I will learn the worst, and
then——’

‘Then,’ said the Frenchman, shrugging his
shoulders significantly, ‘I have done my
duty. I leave the affair in monsieur’s hands,
to be concluded as he thinks fit.’

An hour later they were at sea once more.

Errol Glendenning had completely forgotten Basil.

CHAPTER IV.

THE sea beat stormily against a bold and rugged line of rocks that rose some hundred feet sheer from the bosom of the waters, and then grouped themselves in strange shapes and confused masses, as if hurled and piled together by some Cyclopean hand. Egress or ingress seemed alike impossible. Nothing but fierce eddies and dangerous shoals seemed to defend the shingly banks, yet a boat with a single occupant was making its way through a narrow channel of deep and comparatively smooth water, and finally forced itself through the opposing defences and ran aground amidst the shingle and seaweed.

The occupant was Basil Glendenning. The fact of his guardian's sudden departure had left him stranded on his own resources. The day was calm and peaceful, the sky without cloud, the steamer chartered by Errol Glendenning lay idle.

He went straight to the captain and sai the owner had placed the steamer at his disposal for the day, and something in his calm assurance and authoritative manner had convinced the man of his truth. In any case, he had taken him out to where he had directed, and the boy had gone off in the boat used by his guardian for landing purposes, and declared his intention of exploring the strange groups of islands that had long ago attracted his fancy. What had brought him to this special one he could not say. Something stronger than mere curiosity—a feeling that prompted him to explore this wild and lonely spot, though the captain had assured him that no one ever landed there or lived there : that the island was quite uninhabited, and full of unknown dangers.

To the bold, exploring-loving nature of the English boy nothing could have been more delightful than the thought of proceeding thither. As he stood now on the damp, slippery piles of seaweed, and watched the slow flight of the great gulls, the lightning-flash of finny scales, the whole tremor, and trouble, and mystery of sea-life, here frothy and fierce, here broken into deep, smooth channels of glassy calm, he felt a strange glow of pride and enterprise thrill his veins.

Drawing the light boat high up on the shingle, and fastening it securely in case of the tide rising, he proceeded on his journey of research.

Skirting the base of the cliffs, he came at last to a place where they were broken through by a stretch of water, almost as deep and calm as a lake. Two walls of rough and jagged rocks shut it in on either side ; the sky formed its roof; the sunlight illumined its gloom. Innumerable birds roosted in its crevices and ledges, and flew screaming out now at the intrusion of humanity.

Rough and difficult as the passage was along the margin of the water, Basil followed it undeterred. Light and sure of foot, the slippery rocks and narrow formation of the ground had no terrors for him. For some quarter of a mile he skirted this winding sheet of water ; then he felt the ground rising steadily upwards, and momentarily growing more narrow. Stopping for a moment to examine the appearance of the cliffs above, he saw what looked like a faint track, worn by the tread of feet. It wound upwards in a sloping direction, and seemed to lose itself amidst the coarse grass, and furze, and broom that alone clothed the soil.

'Some one must live here,' he said half aloud, and steadied himself against the wall of rock and looked around.

There was nothing stirring save the birds that screamed and wheeled about below.

After a moment's rest he proceeded up the cliff. The track grew fainter and more difficult to trace, and finally ceased altogether. By this time he had reached the highest point. Standing there he could see all around him, and down into the blue depths beneath. The steamer lay at anchor in a tiny bay close to one of the neighbouring islands. The sun was already low in the western horizon; the birds looked like a flying cloud above the spray and foam of the broken water. He threw himself down on the coarse, scanty grass, and took in all the wild and lovely scene with keen enjoyment.

Rising at last somewhat reluctantly, he took another survey of the limited extent of the island, his eyes keenly alert for a sign of smoke from any fisher-hut that perchance had an inmate in this lonely region.

He could see nothing. The top of the cliffs was apparently broken into hummocks, covered with the same coarse, scanty grass. Brambles and furze were the only vegetation. There, was not a sign of a tree anywhere.

'It is a veritable desert island,' he said to himself, and then started off in the opposite direction to pursue his investigations further. He was too excited, and too heed‧less also, to take account of time. His boat was safe; the steamer would await his pleasure; he did not trouble further. He had reached about the centre of the island, when he paused and drew out his watch. As he did so his glance travelled carelessly round. He looked at the time, then re‧placed the watch in his pocket. The action altogether could not have taken more than half a minute, yet as he again looked round he started, and stood transfixed with an amazement little short of terror, for there, perched on the edge of the cliffs where he

had lately sat, stood a solitary figure out-
lined against the burning colours of the sky,
and the hazy, melting background of sur-
rounding water.

If it had sprung from out of the earth it
could not have appeared more suddenly, and
with more startling effect.

The boy stared, bewildered at its unexpected appearance. It looked so airy and
indistinct that he found himself wondering
if it could be a real, living, human creature.

Seeing that it remained motionless, curiosity prompted him to retrace his steps. He
had come thither with a purpose, and that
purpose might be better served by questioning one of the inhabitants of this apparently
deserted spot.

Throwing off the unreasoning terror that
for a moment had mastered his energies,
he rapidly advanced in the direction of the
motionless figure.

He was within a reasonable distance of it,

when the sound of his steps must have become audible. Suddenly it turned.

The look of terror and strangeness in the face seen in the indistinct light of the rapidly sinking sun, was not yet so strange or so terrifying as the feeling that seemed to curdle the warm blood in Basil Glendenning's veins. For an instant the shock, and surprise, and incredulity held him chained and breathless there.

Then he sprang forward, a cry on his lips, wild, and eager, and passionate as hope and joy could make it.

The echo of that cry, ringing out over the quiet sea, was not more strange and startling than its result.

The figure vanished as suddenly as it had appeared.

The boy stopped as if a blow had struck and paralyzed him. He was quite alone. The burning sun sank like a ball of fire. The track of its passage lay mirrored in a broad line of crimson and gold upon the surface of the sea. The birds still screamed, and called, and wheeled in circling groups among the rocks below.

Vision, dream, reality—what was it that had peopled the empty place into which those young, bewildered eyes gazed strangely, fearfully, doubtingly ?

He could not say. He only knew that he stood on the margin of the rough and rugged headland, and that not another creature was in sight. The little narrow track by which he had ascended, wound its way like a dark ribbon to the water's edge. Not a flutter of dress or echo of step betrayed the existence of the woman he had called on by his own fanciful title—the woman whose fate lay sealed in mystery—whom he had prayed to behold, living or dead, and could have sworn he had so beheld a few brief moments before. With beating heart and throbbing pulse he hurried down the narrow pathway. A false step would have plunged him into that deep, dark lake that wound through the cavernous tunnels of the cliff, but he neither cared for nor thought of that. Suddenly the light faded; the grey chill dusk fell curtain-like over the swelling sea. It was with difficulty that the boy made his way through the vaulted archway —springing recklessly from rock to rock that were swept and damp now with the rising tide.

His boat lay idly rocking on the foam. He saw the water was sweeping rapidly in through the archway by which he had entered. Mechanically he entered the boat, unloosed the rope, and pulled out again to sea. When he was clear of the shoals and currents he rested on his oars, and his eyes swept anxiously the rugged headland where he had lately stood.

A feeling of awe, the like of which he had never known, crept over his bold young heart.

' Is she really dead ? Was it her spirit
that came to tell me so ?' he thought. ' It
could not have been herself, and yet how like
herself it seemed !'

The deepening dusk of the wild December
evening warned him to make his way back
to the steamer. Mechanically he raised the
oars, his strong young arms impelled the
boat over the smooth rolling swell of the
sea.

It was almost dark when he reached the
steamer and stood safe and sound on the
deck.

' I trust monsieur is satisfied with his
island,' said the captain, advancing towards
his young passenger with a smile. ' It is
wild—it is ugly—it is bare. There is no
human creature living on it; is it not so ?'

' I am not quite sure,' said the boy
evasively. ' I hadn't time to see half the
place. I mean to go again to-morrow if the
weather holds.'

'The weather will hold, I do not doubt; but surely monsieur is not in earnest. That is a place of ill-repute. Besides, it is dangerous — most dangerous. They say the sea sweeps through it in several underground caverns. Some day it will be all destroyed —undermined.'

'I mean to go there again to-morrow,' was all the boy answered.

CHAPTER V.

IT was quite early. The mists were just lifting off the sea, the cold, clear, morning light glittered on the rocks and cliffs, the fringe of foam, the great wet piles of sea-weed, the gleam of some white sail far out near the dim horizon line.

Basil Glendenning had risen with the first break of day. He had passed a restless, feverish night, haunted ever by one dream or vision.

He always saw himself standing on the brink of a precipice above a fiercely-break-ing sea. There was a blood-red glow on the water and in the sky. Suddenly a shadow seemed to rise and float before him, beckoning him to follow. But at the first step he felt himself falling, falling into space, with that vanishing form still far beyond his reach, and the veiled face turned towards his own, bathed in the lurid glow of the sunset. He never could see the face with any distinctness, but he seemed to know whose it was, and with the cry of that ever-haunting and beloved name on his lips, he awoke.

Three times he slept, and three times he saw that veiled form, and the lonely cliffs, and the blood-red light of the dying day. At last he could bear it no longer. He sprang up, and dressed, and ordered the boat to be lowered, and floated out on the wide space of heaving water, feeling that there alone could he breathe freely and at ease.

A sort of natural breakwater surrounded the mysterious island which he had visited the previous day. He skirted it cautiously, for the water was rough and dangerous.

Beyond the swirl and rush of its current
the sea was comparatively calm.   He rested
on his oars, and let the boat rock as it would
on the long rolling swell.   The silence, the
pale, drifting mists, the cool, rosy morning
light breaking up the clouds and showing
depths of blue beyond, all soothed and lulled
his feverish energies, and served to banish in
some degree the almost superstitious dread
that he had felt of again approaching the
island.

He set his brain to work at conjectures
that were alike possible and impossible.

His senses were acute, his physical energies
strong and active.   There was nothing
dreamy, idealistic, or romantic about him.
Withdrawn from the influence that had
alarmed and bewildered him, he felt able to
reason more clearly.

' It must have been a human figure,' he
told himself.   ' And, being so, it proves that
the island is inhabited.'

True, the sailors called it uncanny, and told weird stories of things seen and heard there. Not one of the men on board the steamer would have ventured to set foot on its shingly banks, or penetrate its mysterious caves. But here in the cool, glad dawn, amidst the breaking foam, the swelling waves, the flying birds, all fears and superstitions fell from him like a discarded cloak whose weight had been too oppressive.

Cradled in the mighty arms of the great, bright, beautiful sea, he felt strong, and daring, and resolute once more. He made up his mind that he would explore every inch of ground on that deserted spot before he would rest convinced that what he had seen there was not an actual presence.

Cautiously and slowly, he now sought the little channel which had favoured him for a landing-place the previous day. He ran the boat ashore, secured it firmly, and then made his way to the vaulted archway.

The little narrow track was plainly perceptible.   Regarding it scrutinizingly by the
clear, bright daylight, he became convinced
that it had been made by human feet.

He followed it slowly and carefully through
the cathedral-like cave with its roof of cloud
and sky ; by the deep, still waters that had
fretted the walls into strange shapes and
carvings ; and up the sloping, irregular cliff
through piles of rock and gorse and furze, till
once again he stood on the summit.

He drew a long, deep breath as he glanced
around.   The sunlight poured itself in a flood
of liquid gold over the gleaming waters, and
on the coarse herbage and broken hummocks
of the cliff.

As on the previous day, he sat down a
short distance from the cave where he had
seen the mysterious figure.   He was trying
to invent some theory for its disappearance.
When he had rested sufficiently, he approached the spot once more, examining the

ground inch by inch. In one place a huge bush of gorse spread itself amidst the broken fragments and boulders of mingled sandstone and granite that composed the cliffs. He went up to it in the course of his investigations. The soil was soft and broken here, and as he made a spring from one to another of the scattered rocks, he missed his footing, and landed on a little hillock of grass and furze. As his feet touched it, he suddenly felt the earth give way, and he fell straight through into sudden darkness, and to a depth of several feet.

Springing up, bruised and shaken, he found himself in a sloping, underground pathway, that seemed to stretch away into the darkness, and yet was illumined here and there by a slanting ray of sunlight.

Enterprise was strong within him. He shook himself free of the clinging earth, and started forward to explore this passage. It occurred to him suddenly that the disappear-

ance of that mysterious figure was accounted
for now, and that this sloping, irregular way
might lead to some cavern in the midst of the
cliffs.   As his eyes grew accustomed to the
dim light, he saw that it was a natural arched
way he trod, hollowed in the midst of the
cliff, and that at the further end of it was a
dull red glow, which he took to be daylight.
The soil was damp and mossy, the air chill.
He hurried on, his footsteps making no sound
on the soft, moist earth. Suddenly he paused,
and stood still, while a strange, curdling
horror seemed to chill the blood in his
veins, and still the bold, quick beats of his
heart.

He saw before him a small rocky cave.
From the opposite end to where he stood
came a glow of firelight.   The floor was
covered with rough skins ; a few implements
for household use were visible : a charcoal
brazier, a shelf containing books, a wooden
table, some metal pots, a swinging lamp that

was fed with oil and hung from the carved
and fretted roof. But the thing that had
startled and held him spell-bound was a
strange, tall figure, clothed in dusky black
garments, with a flame-coloured girdle round
the waist—a figure weird and awful as that
of any sibyl of old. She stood gazing silently
down at a pile of the same rough skins that
carpeted the floor of the cave, but on them
was stretched another figure—the figure of a
woman, whose white garments gleamed like
light in the dusky shadows.

She lay there as if in deep sleep. The light
fell faintly over her face and on the loose
masses of her unbound hair. Basil, creeping
nearer step by step, with bated breath and
throbbing pulses, saw that the face was indeed the face which had lived in his memory
so faithfully and well for all these weary
months.

Cold and trembling, he rested against the
rocky sides of the tunnel. He saw the dark-

robed woman move softly away, and presently
return with something that looked like an
iron lamp. She placed this on a rough slab of
rock that did duty as a table, and, bending
over it, scattered some powder on the flame.
A dense vapour spread itself around, for a
moment hiding the figure of the strange
woman and the light of the lamp. As it
cleared away, the boy saw that the recumbent
form on the couch of skins had risen to a
sitting position. The face was turned towards
him. The loose, veiling hair fell cloud-like
round its delicate beauty, but the eyes were
closed as if in deep sleep. .

A thrill of joy and expectancy ran through
his veins. He had been right, after all.
Nancette was alive, safe, within call and
reach, at last ! His lips parted ; he was
about to spring forward, when something
stayed him.

The strange woman was speaking. She
stretched out her hands towards the swaying

figure. Imperious, resolute, her voice rang through the stillness. Basil's acquaintance with the French language had considerably improved since he had first known Nancette. Léonie and her father had brought him to a tolerable degree of proficiency. He knew well enough that this woman was speaking in that language, but he could not understand what she said. She seemed to be questioning Nancette, and the girl answered in a slow, measured voice, too faint for Basil's ears. Suddenly she seemed to grow restless; her body swayed, her head turned from side to side.

'There is some one here!' she cried, and rose to her feet, and stretched out her arms to the shadowy passage where, trembling and awe-struck, Basil stood.

He advanced rapidly, fear and wonder forgotten in the joy that swept over sense and soul.

'Nancette!' he cried; 'Nancette!'

As though she had been a dead creature
called back to life, the girl started and
shuddered convulsively, while a low cry of
terror left her lips. Her eyes opened.

Clear, wondering, amazed, they looked
around. The boy threw himself at her feet,
clasping and kissing her dress, her hands, in
a very delirium of joy.

'You are not dead!' he cried; 'you are not
dead! And I have found you—I! Oh,
Heaven be thanked!'

A strong hand seized his shoulder and
almost flung him aside. Springing to his
feet, he found himself confronted by a tall,
majestic figure with pale face and flaming
eyes. Their look, at once fierce and
mystical, thrilled him almost to pain. The
warm current of his blood grew suddenly chill
and cold.

'Why are you here?' she asked.

Her voice was firm, clear, sonorous, unlike
any woman's voice he had ever heard.

With a strong effort he steadied himself, and answered in the same tongue :

'I came to search for her,' pointing to Nancette.

The dark face grew stern and wrathful.

'What is she to you?' she demanded. 'You shall not take her. I claim the right, for I alone can give her back life. The sea brought her to me dead—she is dead still to all and everything I will. Look—see for yourself! She does not know you—she will never know you, or any friend on earth again.'

Basil shuddered with horror as, obeying that imperative gesture, he looked at Nancette. Her eyes were closed; her face looked as if carved in marble. She stood there like a statue—immovable, unmoved—a shape of awe and dread, with no semblance of humanity in the mute lips and sightless eyes.

Rage and fury mastered even the terror in his heart. He sprang towards her.

'What have you done?' he cried passionately. 'She *is* alive—she knew me a moment ago. Nancette, speak—look at me ! You do know me, do you not ? I am Basil, your friend—your little knight, as you used to call me ! Tell me you hear me—you see me ; that you're not—not *dead !'*

But then with a low, shuddering cry he recoiled, for without word or glance the figure swayed, like a statue from its column, and fell on the rough couch, where it lay frozen, and motionless.

' It is as I said,' fell mournfully on his ear ; ' she is dead—dead to all save my will. Dead to earth, and love, and memory, unless I bid her live ! Go your way ; leave us. You are not wanted here.'

He recoiled a step or two, striving manfully to conquer the sense of alarm and horror which this strange being aroused in his soul.

His eyes wandered from that pale face,

with its snow-white hair and flaming eyes, to the silent figure on the rude couch of skins.

‘Whoever or whatever you are,’ he said boldly, ‘I shall not leave here until I take her with me. Dead or living, she belongs to those who have stronger claims than yours. And I am sure she is not dead.’

‘You are sure?’ said the woman with a strange, slow smile. ‘Oh, foolish and ignorant youth, strong in its bold assertion of its own belief! Go to her, touch her, speak to her. If she wakes for you, she may go home freely, unrestrainedly ; but she will not.’

In a sudden wild burst of passionate grief, the boy threw himself down beside that motionless form. He called on her by name, he kissed her cold hands, he implored her to open those close-sealed lids and look at him.

He might as well have implored an image of marble.

She did not stir, she did not look, she did not breathe. The dead itself could not have been more cold and still.

With a smothered cry he rose to his feet.

'Is it sleep or death?' he cried. 'A moment ago she lived—I am sure of it! Her hands were warm—her eyes knew me! What is it you have done?'

Again that slow, cruel smile came over the mystic face.

'She is dead. I told you she was dead. The sea brought her to me, and I took her in here, and by my power I breathe into her the semblance of life. When I withhold my will, she is as you see her now. I have wrested the secrets of nature from their source. I know the occult sciences of life and spirit; I have spent my days in their study. I have a key which opens the inner temple of mystical and spiritual force. To you such things are unknown and un-imagined. I cannot expect you to under-

stand that this form you see here is mine,
by right of those laws which endow it with
spiritual life at my will and desire. To you,
or any other mortal, it is but dead flesh—a
corrupt, soulless mass that the grave must
hide. Go your way, and leave her with me.
Tell those that seek her, she is dead—dead
as any fleshless corruption that they thrust
with loathing from sight and sense!'

Her eyes flamed. Her tall figure seemed
to tower almost to the roof of the cavern.
The dull glow of the ashes shone fitfully on
her dusky robe, her snowy hair, her strange,
wild face.

Basil felt that cold thrill of horror steal-
ing through his veins once more. He looked
from the terrible living face to that still
more terrible dead one.

A numbing fear held his senses in momentary paralysis. He felt speech and action
alike impossible. A drowsy, confused feeling stole the power of will from his brain—

a sense of something fighting with and dominating his mental and physical faculties, was all of which he was conscious.

Involuntarily he stretched out his arms to the stirless form that seemed beckoning him to some shadowy region, cloudy and obscure. Then a great darkness over-whelmed him. He knew nothing more.

CHAPTER VI.

TIME flowed on. The sun was sinking in the west. The sea was tinged with ruddy flame. The air was still, and mild, and without sound, save for the monotonous breaking of the waves upon the bank, or the weird cry of a sea-bird flitting from rock to rock.

When Basil Glendenning awoke, he found himself lying beside his boat on the damp piles of seaweed that covered the shore. He rose to his feet in a dazed and dreamy way. It seemed to him that he had been asleep for long, long hours. A confused sense as of some terrible dream oppressed his brain. He sat down and tried to think clearly and calmly ; but it needed an almost superhuman effort to do so.

Gradually things began to come back to him. And with them the shock and horror of that terrible discovery.

He bent his face on his clasped hands and almost groaned.

'She is dead!' he said over and over again. 'She is dead!'

A sort of longing came over him to see her again—a longing so soul-felt and intense that it seemed to master every other thought and feeling.

Silence fell like the pall of night around him. He scarcely heard the beat of the waves or the sigh of the faint, chill wind that was slowly rising as the sun declined. With his head still bowed in that sorrowful forgetfulness of all save his misery and her fate, he suddenly became conscious of a sound—now far, now close at hand—the rustling of a woman's dress, the faint echo of a woman's footfall. His hands dropped; he looked up. A white figure stood beside him; a face, where terror, pain, suffering, dread, threw varying shadows of emotion, looked back to his own, as the light faded over the purple waters, and the chill breeze swept over the rising tide.

Cold and trembling, the boy started to his feet. He did not speak, he scarcely breathed; he only looked and looked with wide and terrified eyes at the silent figure, and the face turned sadly up to his beneath its veil of shrouding hair.

She came nearer. She laid her hand upon his arm; its touch was like ice.

'Take me away,' she said in a frightened whisper. 'Take me away! You called me —I felt it, even there,' with a shuddering backward look to an outlet in the rocky cliffs. 'You can save me if you will—tell me you will!'

Life, courage, the strength and fierceness of a young lion, seemed to leap like living fire through Basil Glendenning's veins. He seized her hands. He did not waste time in unnecessary words.

In a second he had placed her in the boat, loosed the rope, and pushed off into deep water. Then, seizing the oars, he rowed with strong and rapid strokes through the trough of the swelling waves, and out and on to the glad, free sea beyond.

By sheer instinct he took his way to the steamer. He never spoke, nor did she. With drooping head and sad and wistful eyes she sat there as if carved in stone, but Basil knew well enough she was alive, and that thought made his brain almost reel with joy and triumph.

The steamer was reached, the rope thrown, the ladder lowered.

'Can you get up?' he asked her breathlessly, as he assisted her to keep her position in the rocking boat.

'Yes—yes,' she cried, and seized the rope, and, watched by his eager eyes, ascended quickly and safely to the deck of the steamer.

In an instant Basil followed.

'Weigh anchor!' he shouted to the captain. 'Let us get back to St. Helier's as fast as steam can take us.'

'Monsieur has succeeded, then, in his search,' cried the bewildered Frenchman.

'Yes. Thank Heaven!' said the boy simply; but the tears rose in his eyes as now, all danger past, he looked at the trembling figure by his side.

'Come down into the cabin,' he said gently. 'You are safe now. Neither man, nor woman, nor witch, nor devil shall take you again from me.'

Proud, elated, happy, Basil Glendenning led his precious charge into the cabin, and begged her to lie down and rest while he procured her some refreshment. She was still very cold. He hurriedly gathered together two or three rugs and spread them under and over her ; then he went to the steward and bade him bring some hot tea as soon as possible.

This done, he came and sat down by the girl, and taking her cold hand in his, he began to question her as to the strange events which had sealed her fate in mystery for so long.

Her hand lay listless and passive in his own. She lifted her eyes to his face, but to every inquiry he made, she only answered :

' I do not know.'

For a time the boy smothered his disappointment. He thought she must be weary, spent, harassed, so he ceased to trouble her with questions.

The tea came, and he poured it out, and she drank it in the same passive, obedient manner, and ate the biscuits he gave her, and then lay back again on the pillows, inert and silent, with an apathy towards himself that

made him feel like a stranger, and sent a
curious thrill of fear and disappointment
through his heart.

'Would you like to sleep?' he asked at last.
'We shall be in port in a couple of hours. I
will call you then.'

'Yes,' she said; 'I am very tired. I
thought when one was dead one never felt
tired again, but I do—often.'

The strange words, spoken as calmly and
clearly as if they were all that was reasonable, horrified the boy. He stood there
gazing at her almost in terror.

'You are not dead!' he cried. 'What do
you mean? You are alive—well—safe!
You are going home with me—with Basil.
Don't you remember me, Ladye Nancye?'

The familiar voice, the familiar name,
touched some chord within the numbed
brain, the tortured heart. She rose to a
sitting position. She pushed the veiling
hair from off her brow. As she did so,

Basil saw a red scar traversing the right temple—a cruel, jagged mark that had never disfigured its snowy beauty in the days of old.

A look of pain and bewilderment came into her eyes. She shook her head.

‘ No,’ she said ; ‘I do not remember. I have been dead a long, long time. I do not think the dead remember.’

Then something seemed to stab the boy's heart with pain. The truth flashed across him in one moment of sharp and cruel agony.

All his youth and boyishness seemed to die out of him, leaving him cold and grave, full of serious thought and anxious fears.

He had found Nancette, but she was no longer the Nancette he remembered. Beautiful, sad, harassed by sufferings, cold to all feeling, with no memory of the past, no care for the future—this woman who lay like a fallen statue against the rich and sombre colouring of the rugs, was but the shell, the ghost of the woman he had worshipped with boyish adoration.

He felt choked ; he could not speak ; he could scarcely breathe. He went out of the cabin, and up to the deck, and in the cold, faint gloom he paced to and fro, taking counsel with himself, trying to fathom this mystery—to piece together the puzzle of that broken life, which now was helpless as a child's—to which existence could henceforth be only a negative blessing.

Then grief gave way to fear. Fear for her, her personal safety, her liberty, her peace. If they landed at St. Helier's, and went to an hotel, her strange aspect and conversation would arouse suspicion. A mad-woman ! He shuddered as he thought of it. What could he do ?

The one longing in his mind was to take her home—to hide her from all eyes—to keep this sorrowful and mysterious life safe,

and untroubled, and free from the desecrating
influence of investigation and inquiry.

Could he do this? Was it in any way
possible? He thought of a plan, but it
seemed very hopeless.

He glanced at the sky; it was clear and
faintly lit at intervals by stars. There was
no fog or mist. The wind had died down;
the sea was comparatively calm.

He took courage, and went to the captain
and made his proposition.

It was received with great outcry, as he
expected.

'To England! *Mais, monsieur*, it is impossible!'

'It is quite possible,' Basil said. 'Tide
and weather are in your favour, and I will
give you fifty pounds to do it.'

'Fifty pounds.' The man looked doubtful.
'It is not so much, and your guardian—what
will he say?'

'He will be so pleased at my discovery of

the lady that he will probably give you fifty more,' said Basil coolly. 'Come, make up your mind; you can run us to Southampton in ten or eleven hours. What is that? And you know you have been engaged for another month, and you'll get off it, and be paid all the same. Then think of the service you render to the lady.'

'Ah,' said the Frenchman, laying his hand on his breast; 'there monsieur has me at his feet. I am weak on all points connected with the too charming sex of madame. I and my boat are at her service in proof of my devotion.'

'And fifty pounds,' said Basil with a smile, as he turned away. 'Though how in the name of wonder I'm to get it,' he added to himself, 'is more than I know. I've only a few pounds, and I'll want them for the train. But I'll telegraph to Mrs. Freere the moment we get to Southampton, and we can remain on board till the money comes, and she with it.'

CHAPTER VII.

'I STARTED the instant I had your telegram. I have travelled all night. For Heaven's sake, Basil, tell me what has happened !'

This was Myra Freere's greeting as she stood in the coffee-room of the Royal Hotel, Southampton, in the foggy gloom of the dull December day. Basil Glendenning, grave, pale, anxious, changed out of all likeness to the bold, bright boy she remembered, drew up a chair for her near the window, and seated himself opposite.

' Breakfast will be ready in fifteen minutes,' he said. 'The moment it is over I will take you to her.'

' But why is she not here ?' asked Mrs. Freere wonderingly.

The boy's voice grew lower; he glanced furtively around.

'She is not quite herself,' he said; 'she is —oh, Mrs. Freere, I think she is—mad!'

'Mad!' Myra Freere recoiled in sudden horror. 'What are you saying? It can't be—oh, it can't be!'

'It is,' he said mournfully. 'She has no memory. She doesn't know me, and she persists in saying she is dead. Oh, Mrs. Freere, it is the saddest, most terrible thing you can imagine! I—I sometimes think it would be better if she were what she fancies.'

'Tell me all,' said his companion sharply. 'When and how did you find her?'

He told her the story in brief, plain words, while her pained, bewildered eyes met his own.

'It is like some horrible dream,' she said. 'What can that woman have been?'

'A witch or magician, I'm sure,' said

Basil. 'And it is my belief she has frightened Nancette out of her senses. She has declared her to be dead so long that now she believes it is a fact.'

'I never heard of such a thing. Poor child—poor girl! But perhaps it is 'not as bad as you imagine. How did she bear the voyage?'

'She slept for twelve hours without ever waking. She is as gentle and calm as a child ; but, oh, it makes my heart ache to see her, and hear her! You can't think how terribly changed she is.'

'And your guardian?' asked Myra suddenly. 'Where is he?'

'I haven't the slightest idea,' Basil answered. 'I was to accompany him on the expedition to the Minquiers. When I went to the hotel, I learnt that he and the detective had gone off by the mail-boat to St. Malo. I thought it was a pity the steamer should be idle, so I persuaded the

captain to take me for a cruise. We remained out two days. On the second I
discovered her in that cave, as I told you.'

'But if she came to you, as you describe,
of her own free will, she must have remembered you,' said Mrs. Freere.

He shook his head.

'She may have remembered I had been
there, some feeling may have impelled her to
seek me; but she certainly does not know
who I am, nor does she recollect Owl's Roost.
I have asked her questions till I'm tired.
She has but one answer for all—"I do not
know." It is heart-breaking. I haven't
dared take her to an hotel; I was so afraid
they might see something was wrong, and
insist upon a doctor being called in. That's
why I asked you to bring the money. Did
you?'

'Yes,' said Mrs. Freere; 'though I was
puzzled to think why you wanted so large a
sum.'

' It is to pay the French captain. He brought us here.'

' In Mr. Glendenning's steamer?'

' Yes. He went off, so I didn't suppose he wanted it. It will go back at once now I can pay for our passage. If Mr. Glendenning has come back to Guernsey it will be all right. The captain can tell him why I did this. I can write, you know, and explain. Why, Mrs. Freere, you're not going to faint! How white you look!'

' Do I?' she said with evident effort. ' No; I am not faint—only——'

' I know,' he said in a low, troubled voice. ' You think it is worse even than death—so did I at first. But she may recover. People do, don't they? She is just as gentle and sweet as ever, only she has this strange fancy. But if she has lived all these months with that terrible woman, I'm not surprised at her losing her senses. She nearly terrified me out of mine.'

'It is the most extraordinary tale I ever heard,' said Mrs. Freere thoughtfully. 'I almost dread seeing her. I wonder if she will know me? I think we must have a doctor to see her in London, Basil. He could tell us whether there is hope for her recovery.'

'But if he should say she must go to—to—— Oh, Mrs. Freere, I can't bear to think of it!'

'He would not say so,' she answered gently. 'Unless there was reason to fear a stage of violence. Even then we could have an attendant for her ourselves. But I wish —oh, I wish Errol were here!'

'He has never troubled much about her— that I know very well,' said Basil indignantly. 'If he had behaved like a proper-minded husband, she would never have come to this awful state.'

Myra Freere looked sadly at the young, indignant face.

'My dear,' she said, ' you do not know the story. You cannot judge between them. He has told me all. It is very pitiful—very sad, and this will make it worse.'

The boy sighed, and turned away. Just then the waiter entered with the breakfast. They spoke no more on the subject while they made some poor pretence of drinking the coffee, and eating the hot rolls and ham and eggs Basil had ordered.

It was a relief to both when they were out in the open air—dull and murky as it was.

A few minutes afterwards, Myra, with beating heart and trembling limbs, stood in the presence of the woman she had loved so dearly, and mourned so faithfully all these weary months.

Nancette was sitting in the cabin gazing wistfully before her—her hands folded, her whole expression one of passive listlessness.

Myra felt the scorch of tears in her eyes

as she looked at the changed, pathetic face ;
she placed her hands on the girl's shoulders
and gazed longingly at her.

'Nancette,' she said gently—'dear Nancette, how glad I am to see you again !'

A strange, clouded look came over the
quiet face.

'Are you dead, too ?' she asked.

Myra's hands dropped.

Prepared as she was for the shock, it terrified and pained her.

'Don't you remember me ?' she asked at
last, when she had regained her self-command.

Nancette looked at her and shook her
head.

'No,' she said ; 'I remember nothing of
when I was alive except pain—a long, long
dull ache. But the waters covered it, and
they swept it all away. There is no more
now.' She clasped her hands on her bosom
and looked up at the pitying face. 'Sit

here,' she said, 'by me, and I will tell you how I died.'

Myra seated herself with a heart-broken look at Basil.

He turned aside.

The sound of that plaintive voice wrung his heart whenever he heard it.

'I was out in a boat,' said the girl presently; 'it grew dark, and I heard the thunder rolling in the sky. There was water everywhere. I liked it. I did not mind. I loved to feel the dashing waves, the salt, soft spray—to see the lightning chasing its own flashes through the black sky. The boat carried me on—I did not care whither. It grew darker and darker; the gusts of wind were like blows. The boat rocked and reeled, but it flew on swiftly and more swiftly. There had been someone in it with me. I do not know when I first found I was alone. Then came a bright flash as of flame. I saw huge rocks towering above me.

I saw a great wave curling upward—then a weight as of falling water was upon me. My eyes closed. All was dark—dark—dark. That was death !'

She paused for a moment and put up her hand to the cruel, disfiguring scar.

' They are very kind,' she went on, ' to the dead. I was warm and sheltered, though the earth was cold about me. Sometimes I seemed to wake, and there were strange forms around and about, and one seemed to rule them all. At her will we woke, or slept, or dreamt, or moved. I had many strange dreams. She told me I was dead. She taught me strange things. I could go to all parts of the earth Space and distance were as nothing. I was afraid of her, but I knew I must obey her. I could sleep, breathe, move, but as she wished. Sometimes she took me to seas of blood and bade me cross them, and to strange temples, where the dead worshipped the powers of good and

evil. I learnt and saw the immeasurable
mysteries which are the sources of life, and
death, and fate. Then suddenly, one day,
something called me back. Her power was
strong, but this was stronger. Her force
held me in sleep, but this had power to
awaken me. I found myself alone. The
shapes and shadows had all fled, and the
voice that woke me summoned me to meet it,
and I left the earth that had buried me and
went on and on till I found who had spoken.
Then I saw the sea once more—the cruel sea
that had taken my life—but I was not
afraid, and the woman was not there, and the
voice led me on by force and strength of its
will that had vanished hers. I follow it still.
But when it questions I cannot answer, for I
know that I am dead, and the dead lose all
memories of the living. That is why they
are happy.'

Her voice ceased, like a low and plaintive
strain of music that had come to an end.

Again her hand wandered to her forehead with that pathetic gesture. Something seemed trying to force itself into the clouded brain, but it escaped and left her disturbed and restless instead of calm.

Gently Myra Freere approached and touched the wandering hands.

'Will you come with me?' she said. 'I will ask you no more questions, but I will try to make you happy.'

She rose at once.

'You must take me,' she said, 'where the woman cannot follow. She troubles me.'

'She shall not trouble you again, rest assured,' said Myra soothingly. 'Come.'

CHAPTER VIII.

FROM place to place—from town to town, Errol Glendenning pursued the shadowy phantom evoked by the words of Paul Lihou.

The landlord of the hotel at St. Malo confirmed in every particular the story of Madame Lamontaine. On the morning of that special day, two people, answering to the description of Pierre de Volens and Nancette, had landed by the mail-boat; the boat had been delayed by the storm. The lady was ill and weak, and went at once to her room, where she remained all day. They left by the night-train for Rouen. That was all he knew.

Errol Glendenning listened in rigid silence, with perfect self-control. Yet his heart was rent and torn by anguish. The mockery of his marriage stood out in cruel, vivid colours.

When he had heard all, he simply waved the garrulous landlord aside. Perhaps his faith in his glib story might have been shaken had he known that the man was a brother of Madame Lamontaine—that a certain letter from that lady rested warm and safe in the breast-pocket of the garrulous landlord's coat, containing certain instructions to be carried out and liberally paid for.

But knowing nothing of such matters, Errol Glendenning had to bear his suffering and shame in silence that gave no sign of self-betrayal, that Paul Lihou involuntarily admired.

'What shall we do next, monsieur?' he asked. 'Follow them?'

'Yes,' said Errol; 'I must have actual

proof with my own eyes that they are together. We will go on to Rouen.'

Rewarding the landlord for his information with a generosity that made him open his Breton eyes to the utmost, they left St. Malo and proceeded to Rouen. There, however, the traces grew indistinct. ' It was so long ago ;' ' so many ladies and gentlemen had been coming and going all through the summer ;' the name of Pierre de Volens was certainly not in the books.'

These and similar vague statements were all that could be obtained.

From Rouen they proceeded to Louviers, and thence to Paris.

Paris is rather a vague address ; but it is also the very home and centre of a perfect system of criminal investigation.

With infinite labour did Lihou toil through hotel and lodging-house registers and directories, and at last he discovered the name he sought.

Accompanied by Glendenning he went to the address—not an aristocratic one, in the Rue Crozatier. A fresh disappointment awaited them. M. de Volens had lived there for two months, from July to September of that year, but he had left at the end of September for Vienna.

' Alone ?' inquired the detective.

' Quite alone,' was the answer.

' And the apartment—had that also been occupied by M. de Volens only ?'

' But, yes—certainly,' answered the *concierge.* ' Monsieur had been ill most. of the time—of a fever, brought on by cold and exposure in a terrible storm while crossing that too atrocious Channel. As soon as he was well enough to travel, he had left Paris. He stated that he had an appointment— official or government—in Vienna. No more had been heard of him since.'

Half faithless, yet half relieved, Errol Glendenning turned away, and walked with rapid, uneven steps down the slushy, dirty street, and turned into the neighbouring boulevard.

A drizzling rain was falling, melting the snow that had fallen the previous day. The mud was nearly ankle-deep. But the fever in his veins, the restless desire for action or movement of some sort, prevented him from engaging any of the loitering cabs that seemed entreating a fare.

' You see it is all ended now,' he at last exclaimed, as he glanced at Lihou's gloomy face. ' She has not been here—that is certain, or else we were on the wrong track.'

The detective felt his dignity impugned.

' The evidence is strong, monsieur, as far as Rouen,' he said. ' But he may have left her, or she him, before he came to Paris.'

Glendenning was silent. For the first time doubt seized him. He felt weary of this humiliating chase—this will-o'-the-wisp that escaped him at every turn. He said no more to Lihou, who also seemed absorbed in speculations and theories. When they reached their hotel he went at once to the reading-room. Paul Lihou, however, took himself off to see some of his colleagues.

Glendenning felt ill and worn; his limbs ached, and his head seemed in a whirl. Since he had left Guernsey, he had been in a constant state of repressed excitement, his nerves strung to the most acute tension, his physical and mental energies taxed to the uttermost. Now the long strain seemed to snap.

Utterly exhausted and worn out, he sank down on a chair by the window, wondering, in a vague, dim way, what was the matter with him. His clothes were damp with rain, his boots soaked with the mud and slush of the melted snow. But he felt he had not the energy to change either one or other.

The voice of a waiter roused him at last. He was bringing in a pile of journals and papers. Seeing *Galignani* on the top of the heap, Errol mechanically stretched out his

hand for it.   His eyes glanced in a dull, unseeing fashion over the English news, the
political and Parisian notes.   Then a strange
dizziness came over him.   The lines and
columns seemed to run into a strange, blurred
mass.   With an effort he roused himself as
one does when sleep is creeping unawares
over the brain at an inadvertent moment.
He looked round the room.   It was quite
deserted.   It was warmed, and lit, and com-
fortable.   A deep-cushioned lounge stood by
the fire.   Impelled by some idea of reaching it,
he rose to his feet, the paper still in his hand.

Again that dizziness and drowsiness seized
him.   He shook it off with an angry and
resentful effort, and reached the chair, and
sat down.   As he did so his eyes for a
moment rested on a column in the paper he
still grasped in his hand.

Something familiar in the words arrested
his notice.   He found himself reading them
again and again :

'*If this should meet the eye of Errol Glen-denning, Esq., of Owl's Roost, he is entreated to return home at once. News.*'

'Return home!' 'News!' What could it mean? Only that something had been heard of—of whom? Who was it he was trying to seek? The thought and the name escaped him. That strange dull drowsiness swept over him once more. Things began to array themselves before him in a blind, disconnected way. Once he heard himself laugh. The sound was so horrible and so startling that it forced him to sit up and look half-fearfully around, in case anyone else heard it. But he was still alone. Then something seemed clanging and beating in his brain. The noise deafened him. He held up his hand entreatingly.

'Don't!' he cried with piteous entreaty. 'You stun me. I can't hear; and I must go home; they want me—*she* wants me. I must go home—I must go home.'

Between the faltering words he had risen
to his feet, with some vague idea of getting
out of the room and out of the house. But
ere he reached the door he stumbled like a
helpless child. With one last effort to keep
himself from falling, he seemed to plunge into
a great black void.

CHAPTER I.

December 29*th*, 187–.—Back again at Owl's
Roost. Back again, and more sad at heart
than when I left it.

It seems strange that Basil has succeeded
where we all failed. Strange that he should
have found our poor lost girl. Once he
saved her life. Again he has rescued her
from a fate that was but death in life. The
more I hear from her of that strange creature
who has held her captive for these past
months, the more weird and horrible the
story seems.

As far as I can judge, Nancette, on that
fateful day, found she had missed the ex-

cursion-steamer, and walked for some distance
along the shore, and away from the harbour.
Presently she saw a boat lying idly in one
of the little nooks between the harbour and
l'Ancresse Bay. A stout fisher-lad was mind-
ing it. She asked him to take her out on
the sea, and he did so.

They went towards the Autelet Rocks.
A stronge breeze was blowing from the land,
and the boat flew along very rapidly. They
were a long way from Guernsey when the
storm broke, and the lad thought it best to
make for the nearest port. From her description he must have tried the water-passage
between Gouliot and Brecqhon. But the
force of wind and water were too strong to be
combated. The boy was swept away, and
she nearly shared the same fate.

From this point she loses all coherence.
She declares she was drowned, that she
found herself buried in the earth, that a
strange shape stood before her, and called

her, and sent her here and there at will, sometimes chaining her in long sleeps, sometimes sending her spirit on strange and mystic errands.

I began to think of all the curious things I had read and heard—especially in America —about mesmerism, magnetism, and clairvoyance. I knew there was a race of beings to whom occultism and mysticism were actual sciences, studied to their deepest depths, absorbing every interest of life and soul. Had Nancette met some such being, and fallen under her influence, or was it only another delusion of the poor, ill-balanced brain?

Then came Basil's story, corroborating her own. He had found her in a cave, on one of those dreary, desolate, rocky islands that are supposed to be uninhabited, and lie in a dark, forbidding chain between the French coast and the Douvres.

The woman who lived in this cave had an evil reputation, and was supposed to be a witch. None of the fisher-folk would approach it, which was naturally the very reason why Basil determined to explore it first.

Accident divulged the hiding-place where the solitary creature lived and studied her strange arts. He had been terrified by her, and almost convinced that Nancette was dead, as she declared. Then, suddenly and unexpectedly, the girl herself appeared before him. Seenig her alive and safe, and away from that terrible creature in the cave, the boy's first and only thought was to get her on board the steamer that was waiting his return. She made no resistance. In the same way he brought her safely to Southampton, where he telegraphed to me to come at once, as she was found.

I came at once, totally unprepared for the dreadful disclosure he had to make—totally unprepared to hear my poor girl greet me as a stranger.

And now we have brought her here. She seems to have some vague memory of the place, but it is a painful and uneasy one. She seems confused and bewildered when we question her; but she will talk freely and unrestrainedly of the events of what she terms her death.

I have had the opinion of a doctor celebrated for his treatment of mental cases. He says Nancette's brain has been numbed by some severe shock, following on the blow that cut open her head when she was dashed against the rock.

The shock, of course, must have been dealt by the Mystic, who has kept her all this time in the belief that she is dead.

The doctor seemed doubtful of her recovery. His opinion was that another shock would either startle the brain once more into activity, or kill her outright. Such an opinion alarmed me terribly. But as time goes on I begin to doubt its accuracy.

Mental disorders are, of all others, the most difficult to analyse and pronounce upon. Even the greatest authorities sometimes find themselves defied and defeated by a simple natural force, set in motion by simple natural causes, of which they have taken no count because of their very simplicity. My opinion is that if anyone can do Nancette good, or wean her disordered fancy from its fixed belief, it will be Basil.

With him she is always gentle and calm. His power it was that broke asunder the magnetic chains of that powerful sleep, and brought her to his side. He it is for whom she looks and watches in a vague, restless fashion, that his voice or step at once dispels and calms. He it is on whom her own spirit depends, and by whom it seems led to calmer and more rational channels of thought.

In the interest of the girl and of Errol I have resolved that he shall remain at Owl's

Roost, at least for a time, or until Errol himself returns here.

Where he is I cannot imagine. From the hour he left Guernsey I have had no word of his doings. I have written there again and again, but to no purpose. The landlord of the hotel states that he has not yet returned from St. Malo, and all my letters are waiting until he does, or gives me a new address.

One day, Basil offers a bright suggestion. He says :

' Advertise in *Galignani's Journal.* He is sure to see that, wherever he is.'

I at once send to the London agents, and make the necessary arrangements for putting in an advertisement, and keeping it there for a month or more.

Three weeks have passed ; there has been no result.

January 20th.—Stewart has gone back to

school alone.   I could not part with Basil.
His patience and gentleness pass all belief.
He has such hopes of Nancette's recovery
that he inspires me with the same.   All the
boyishness, and mischief, and wildness seem
to have left him.   He is, to all intents and
purposes, a man now, strong, capable, reasoning—a young epitome of Errol himself, whom,
indeed, he strangely resembles.

But the dark curtain is still drawn over
Nancette's mind and memory, and the dull,
monotonous winter days pass on, each like
the other in its dreariness and gloom.

January 30*th.* — A month has passed.
Sadly indeed has the New Year dawned
for us.   There is still no word from Errol.
I am growing alarmed, accustomed as I am
to his fits of absence and silence.   Can anything have happened ?   Can he be ill ?

He has not returned to Guernsey, and I
know no way of making inquiries at St.

Malo. Basil might go, but then I fear the effect of his absence on Nancette.

Day by day she clings to him more. She walks, drives, and rides as he dictates. Her bodily health is marvellously improved. She has gained flesh and colour, and physical strength; but her memory is still void, her delusion still unshaken.

January 31*st.* *Midnight.* — A strange suggestion has shaken me to the very soul. Basil has been sitting here talking to me for the last hour. The boy, it appears, has been studying Swedenborg, Boehme, and Heaven knows how many other dreadful writers.

I call them dreadful, despite their genius, for to my woman's mind there is something terrible in this inner research of what is veiled and secret—in lifting the veil from the spiritual temple and analysing its essence, its sources, its capabilities for the develop-

ment of occult powers. Filled with a mis-
cellaneous quantity of information on these
subjects, Basil proceeds to propound to me
a theory of his own.

It is evident, he says, that the woman, or
Mystic, or whatever she was, chained Nancette's mental faculties into a sleep for certain
purposes of her own. Therefore, she alone
can unchain them.

In his belief, a certain portion of Nancette's brain, or spirit, has been lulled into
a sleep from which it cannot awaken except
by the will of the person who has magnetised
it. He quotes strange stories and authorities
for this theory, showing he has studied mystical literature to some advantage. To my
matter-of-fact mind these ideas seem pre-
posterous, and even the authorities he quotes
do not succeed in convincing me.

His idea now is to go himself to this
woman, and beg her to cure Nancette. The
scheme is so bold and so extraordinary that

it almost takes my breath away. But I oppose it strongly. In the first place, I fear that the boy's absence might have an ill effect upon Nancette ; in the next, I dislike the idea of being mixed up with anything mystical and uncanny, and inexplicable to common-sense and ordinary reason.

I don't believe in mesmerism and magnetism. They seem to imply a morbid condition of mind, worked upon by superstition, or forced into a certain groove by power of a stronger mind, equally ill-conditioned. Nervous and hysterical people might possibly be led to believe in such matters, but I most assuredly never could.

If it were not for Basil's assurance to the contrary, I should be inclined to think the story of the Woman of the cave a myth altogether. His testimony, however, agrees so well with that of Nancette that I feel compelled to give it credence. The idea, however, of appealing to this mysterious being fills me with horror. I point out to Basil that she might choose to re-assert her power over the girl, instead of releasing her from its baneful effects. In that case, we should be worse off than before.

'In my own belief,' I said, 'you have broken her spell by putting the sea between you, and I really cannot consent to inviting a Witch of Endor here as a guest.'

So the boy gives up the argument, and goes away, unconvinced. I think his new studies are unsettling his brain, and I advise him strongly to put them aside; but they are too absorbing and interesting—so he says.

February 5th.—Nancette does not care now for books, or work, or even music. She likes being out in the open air, but no place she visits—even the sea—seems to recall her past life, or aid her in picking up the dropped threads of memory.

I am obliged to deny her to visitors for fear the secret of her condition should be revealed. We are gradually dropped and isolated, and I fancy Owl's Roost begins to have an evil reputation. Once or twice I have been to church, but it is plain to see that I am also ostracised, so I give up doing so, and even cease to wonder that our venerable pastor does not favour us with his spiritual visits any longer. The voices of the female members of the congregation are evidently too strong for him, poor man! We must consider ourselves 'cut' by the whole county.

Oh, if Errol would only write or come !

CHAPTER II.

February 10*th.*—Nancette has developed a strange fancy the last few days. She sits in the boys' old play-room, and gazes for hours at the picture there of the 'Ladye Nancye' — the picture that so strangely resembles herself, and by whose title Basil has always called her.

We do not disturb her. We are in hopes that it may prove even one link in the broken chain that her mind seems powerless to gather or connect.

After looking at it for a long time to-day, she turned to me and said softly:

'That was I—when I lived.'

I did not know what to say. The assertion was so calm and confident.

' I forget my story,' she went on presently.
' I was always watching for someone, I think.
There were trees, and a long, dark road, and
the sky was red ; but he never came.'

My heart began to beat violently. Was
memory returning ? It seemed so, for she
was really relating the very story of the
picture.

'He never came.' Was it her husband of
whom she spoke ?

I still sat there silent. I feared to speak,
lest it might break the delicate strands of
that invisible chain which linked her wandering thoughts to a real memory at last.

She pressed her hands against her brow in
the old bewildered, painful way.

'I think,' she said, 'I have lived twice.
I seem to hear someone telling me so.'   .

She turned and looked at me.

'Was it you ?' she asked.

'No, dear,' I said gently. 'Perhaps it was
Basil.'

She shook her head.

‘No,’ she said slowly. ‘It was a child, I think—a little child. He’—and she looked from side to side of the dreary old room—·‘he used to be here.’

My thoughts flew to Stewart. Was it possible that she missed him ?’

‘He had gray eyes,’ she said suddenly—· ‘gray eyes, and a pale, wistful face.’

‘That was Stewart,’ I said. ‘You remem-· ber him ?’

The dull, clouded look came over her face· again.

‘Do the dead remember ?’ she asked· wistfully.

It was the old helpless question and the· old helpless look. I sat there watching her, sick at heart with fresh disappointment. She· remained quite still, only looking ever and anon at the picture in its tarnished frame, and seeming to find in it an absorbing subject for her thoughts.

Gradually the day began to close in. I lit the lamp and stirred the fire to a brighter blaze. While doing this my back was turned to the door. I heard no sound of it being opened or shut, but when I looked round Nancette had disappeared.

Startled and alarmed, I immediately rushed to the door, and looked down the corridor. She was not in sight. We never left her alone at any time. Basil or myself were always with her. So I immediately started in pursuit. I looked in the library and in our usual sitting-room; but she was not there. Then I went upstairs to her bedroom. It was empty. Basil was out, so I sought old Deborah, and asked her if she had seen her mistress.

' No,' she said; ' she has not been here to-day.'

Growing somewhat uneasy, I threw a shawl round me and went out on to the terrace in front of the house.

It was quite dusk now, and a difficult matter to distinguish anything.

A footstep suddenly sounded. I sprang eagerly forward, calling her name. I found myself face to face with Basil.

'Have you seen Nancette?' I cried wildly. 'She has left the house. I can't find her.'

'Left the house! By herself! Are you sure?' he exclaimed.

'Yes,' I said, and hurriedly related the particulars of our conversation.

'If she has got that in her head,' he said excitedly, 'I can find her. I told her the story.'

Then, without another word, he was speeding down the avenue, leaving me standing there more puzzled and bewildered than ever.

It might have been half an hour, or more, before Basil returned. She was with him.

He whispered me to make no remark, so I merely took off the white shawl she had thrown over her head and shoulders, and put her in her usual low seat by the fire. In a few moments she went off into a deep sleep, her head lightly pillowed on her slender white hand, as she lay back in the chair, her beautiful profile looking pale and wan in the dull glow of the wood fire.

Then Basil beckoned me aside.

'She thinks,' he said, 'that she is the Ladye Nancye of the picture. She was watching in the avenue, just like the story says the—the other one did. Oh, Mrs. Freere, she must have remembered what I told her nearly three years ago! Her mind has gone back to the time she came here. Isn't that something? Who knows if in time she won't recall it all, and then——'

He paused. We looked at one another in silence. The same thought throbbed in both our hearts ; we did not need to speak it.

The next day, at the same hour, Nancette did the same thing.

We followed her as she sped down the avenue and paced to and fro under the tall elm-trees, watching in a strained, intent fashion for someone to enter the closed gates. After half an hour's vigilance she seemed to grow weary, and we approached and took her unresistingly back to the house. Then, as on the previous day, she laid herself down on the couch and went off into a deep sleep.

To me this sudden phase of her disease seems hopeful. Memory is slowly waking. I believe that in some dim way she is watching for Errol—that some faltering thought keeps urging her to look for his return.

My resentment at his absence and silence are slowly resolving themselves into despair. My hands seem tied. I can tell him nothing, and do nothing. Only be patient and silent here, with this broken mind for companionship, and my sad and hopeless thoughts as friends.

The third day, and again, for the third time, Nancette took her way to the avenue as the dusk was falling. I attempted to stay her, but she grew so restless, and seemed so unhappy, that for fear of ill-effects I at last let her slip away as if I did not notice it.

When she returned this time, however, there was a strained, eager look in her eyes I had not before noticed.

She drank the tea I gave her, and then, as before, threw herself back on the couch, and went off into that sudden, strange sleep.

Basil and I drew our chairs up to the fire, and sat there talking in low, hushed voices. Strangely enough, the boy again alluded to his idea about the mysterious woman. He had been reading some more books, and evolving some more theories.

'I am sure,' he said, 'if we could persuade her to unseal the brain, to lift the mystical weight from the spirit-forces, Nancette would recover.'

'My dear boy,' I said, 'if you go on at this rate your own brain will give way. I think you would be better at school.'

'Yes,' he said; 'no doubt. But I am determined to cure her first. Mrs. Freere, I wish you would read——'

'I will read nothing,' I said obstinately. 'Those books only bewilder and terrify. They take away everything, and give nothing.'

'I don't mean a book,' he said. 'I mean a letter.'

'A letter!' I said. 'From whom?'

'From Léonie,' he said gravely, and took a thick packet from out of his pocket, and handed it to me.

As I touched it the figure on the couch stirred uneasily, a low moan as of pain left

her lips. We both looked at her. Basil
went forward, and laid his cool hand gently
on her forehead.

The moaning ceased. Her breathing grew
gentle and placid once more. She looked
like a lovely statue lying there in that deep
repose.

Basil then returned to his seat. I opened
the letter. I saw it consisted of many sheets
closely written. The flames were leaping
merrily in the wide grate. I bent towards
them, and began to read:

'La Rocque, Guernsey, January 28th.

'DEAR BASIL,

'Your letter has surprised me very
much. We all thought you were with your
guardian all this time. I am glad—so glad
you found Madame Nancye.

'Your tale reads like a story of witches
and the black art; but I suppose it is all
true. I am sorry that your visit was cut

short ; but, of course, I see quite plainly that
you could not have acted differently. What
you say of Madame's loss of memory is very
sad, and your extraordinary theories about it
make me wonder if your mind is not also a
little *dérangée.* Be not offended that I say
so. I have not, in the course of my studies,
ever taken up such strange works as those
you speak of; but I shall certainly try and
get them.

' . . . I broke off here yesterday, as *maman*
wished me to go out on an errand. I thought
I would come home by our favourite bay. I
was walking along at my ease—not in any
haste, you understand—when suddenly I saw
before me the figure of a woman. She was
all in black, and very tall ; her hair was as
white as snow ; her eyes were large and
wild.'

I started. The letter dropped from my
lap. I looked up and met Basil's eyes.

'The same woman?' I said, below my breath.

He nodded.

'Read on,' he said.

'I don't know where she sprang from so suddenly,' went on the letter; 'I only know that there she was. I stopped and looked at her, and she looked at me. She spoke first.

' "You live here?" she said.

'I answered simply :

' "Yes, madame."

' "Can you tell me," she asked, "if anything has been heard on the island of a woman dressed in white ? *A mad woman.*"

'I started ; I thought of your letter and of Nancette. I answered evasively :

' "I am not acquainted with anyone on the island," I said. "I have certainly not heard of such a person being here. You had better inquire of the police."

'Then I tried to move on. I felt uncomfort-

able.   She motioned me to remain still; her
eyes seemed to pierce me.

' "You have a friend," she said; "he is
young, and bold, and strong of will.   Tell him
he has vanquished me once; but my turn
will come.   He has stolen the empty shell;
but I have the jewel.   He has the dead body;
but the spirit is with me.   Some day his
vigilance will relax—the force of his presence
will be withdrawn.   Then, at a word, the
body will return to me to claim what I withhold.   His power is strong now—the power
of a pure, strong, unselfish love.   But against
it I employ the power of a great and all-
embracing knowledge.   Sea and space divide
us; but my will could traverse them did I
wish.   But I am content to wait.   Tell him
I am content to wait."

' Now, Basil, you will scarcely believe that
by the time she had finished this harangue I
was really frightened.   It was growing dark.
I was all alone, and this strange, wild crea-

ture terrified me with her looks and gestures.
Every word she said seemed to burn itself
like fire into my brain. I could not forget
them, nor could I speak. When she ceased,
however, she moved slowly away, and went
down to the water's edge, and seemed to fade
darkly and indistinctly into the gathering
shadows of the falling night, and the hazy
outlines of rock and cliff. As for me, I simply
flew over the shingle and sand, and never
slackened speed till I reached home.

'The good *maman* was at vespers. I was
glad she did not see me; I looked so strange.
I sat down at once and added all this to my
letter. What do you think of it? Certainly
now I shall read Swedenborg and those other
authors. I close this to catch the post. If I
hear or see any more of the strange woman I
will write at once.

'LÉONIE.'

As I finished, another low moan from

Nancette attracted my attention. I looked at her. She was sitting up ; her eyes were wide open, but with no look of actual sight within them. She put her hands to her head, then let them fall with a despairing gesture.

Again the low moaning cry escaped her pale and quivering lips.

As I sprang hastily up, the scattered sheets fluttered into the wide fireplace, and in a second were blazing fiercely with the wood. Basil and I were both too much alarmed by Nancette's appearance to attempt to rescue them. We approached her, not daring to speak. We could see that the look in her eyes was not one of reason or sense.

Quite suddenly, as the last scrap of paper fluttered blackened and charred on to the piled gray ashes beneath the grate, the strained, terrible look died out of those unseeing eyes. With a deep sigh of relief she sank back on the cushions. The lids closed. A faint murmur stirred her lips.

'It is gone,' she said. 'Ah, the relief, the joy!'

Basil looked at me with a strange triumph on his face.

'It was the letter,' he said; 'it is burnt, and she has recovered. Perhaps you'll tell me you don't believe in magnetism now?'

CHAPTER III.

Midnight.—I have copied Léonie's letter from memory. It is strange that every word of that woman's speech seems mentally photographed on my brain.

Reviewing the whole facts of Nancette's seizure, I cannot but believe it is no ordinary one. Whoever or whatever this Woman is, she evidently found in our poor, heart-sick girl a good subject for her strange powers. She forged chains for her memory that bound her only to remember as she willed. She swept away the past, lest its powers should thwart her own. She dealt with her, in fact, as if she were an entirely irresponsible being, given over body and soul to her will.

It seems to me, however, that she reckoned too much on her absolute control over the girl. The force of another will, a will strong and pure, by reason of a pure love, thwarted her purpose, baffled her power, and drew the victim away from the baleful spell of her presence. A force mightier than magnetism had all unwittingly come into play when she least expected it. I think Basil's very unconsciousness but added to his influence over Nancette. As long as she was with him, near him, I felt she was comparatively safe, but then reason prompted me to ask how long such a state of things could be possible. Tenderly and reverently as the boy loved her, we could not expect him to waste his life and energies in such a slavish fashion. It would be too cruel to him.

*   *   *   *   *

The door between our rooms is open. I can see the bed, and see Nancette's figure lying there in the placid calm of deep slum-

ber. There is no egress from her room
except through mine, and I am in the habit
every night of locking the door and putting
the key under my pillow. Besides this, my
sleep is never sound now; the slightest
movement awakes me. The uncertainty
caused by her state and mental condition keeps
me in perpetual dread. I have had high
bars put to both our windows, and yet, even
with these safeguards, and the key in my own
possession, I never feel that Nancette is safe.

Very often I sit here till daybreak, watching her : oftener still, thinking over the sad
blow in store for Errol when he returns.

We often speak of the irony of fate. I
seem to recognise the full bitterness of that
phrase at last.

That I—I, of all women—should be thrust
into such a position—the keeper of this poor,
ill-fated, friendless creature, who is as de-
pendent as a child on patience and on love!

I shudder at the dreary prospect, at the long, hopeless struggle before me ; but never for one single moment do I contemplate relinquishing my charge ; never do I waver in that resolution, made when first Errol Glendenning told me his sad story—to be the friend of both ; to strive, so long as it lies in human power, to smooth the hard path, restore the lost faith, help him to happiness, and love, and joy once more.

The task was hard before—it seems almost impossible now — yet I do not despair. Strange and mysterious as are the two destinies I love so dearly, sad and bewildering as seems the tangled web of their severed lives, I yet feel the assurance of help, the hope of better, brighter hours. Surely I am strong enough and brave enough to battle on still.

I have been reading that letter over again ; one sentence in it makes me uneasy. It is a sentence spoken by the Woman : 'Some day his vigilance will relax, the force of his presence will be withdrawn ; then, at a word, the body will return to me, to claim what I withhold.'

There is something horrible about the idea of this creature holding back the spiritual essence which could once again restore light and reason to our poor, distraught girl.

Yet, if she has such a power, would it not be better to act on Basil's advice and either try, or persuade, or force her to exercise it ? The only thing is, perhaps she might be unpersuadable, or she might use it for her own bad ends, and take Nancette from us.

AN INTERLUDE OF LETTERS.

February 8th, 187—.

DEAR LÉONIE,

- Your letter was very welcome. The part about the Woman in Black startled me very much. I am sure she is the woman of whom I told you, and who lived on that strange island where I discovered my Lady Nancye. I am sorry to say she is no better. Mrs. Freere thinks I had best remain at Owl's Roost until we hear from my guardian, for Nancette is fond of me, and will generally do whatever I wish. This leads me to suppose that I have some sort of influence over her.

31—2

Her memory is still a blank; but lately she
has shown signs of remembering one incident
of her old life here, and that gives me hope
that in time she will remember others. I
read a great deal now. I want, as I told
you before, to get at the mysterious ' something ' which wraps this poor darkened
mind. It is a longing, like thirst. Oh, to
set her free — to make her happy! I
don't think my life would want anything
else.

There's no doubt that we don't any of us
think half enough of these mystic and im-
portant matters. We just live out our lives
from day to day, never troubling about
the source of happiness, the capabilities for
thought, or action, or good or evil, that make
up, after all, our real nature. I believe, if
one thinks solemnly and seriously about
these matters and intensifies one's will, so
that one can look far below the mere fact of
living, and moving, and breathing, one is

capable of a strange power—an insight, as it were, into things never dreamt of.

I don't express myself well, I know ; but it is always hard for me to put my thoughts into writing. You have often said I was stupid, and not a bit imaginative. I know that is so, and I am afraid this will sound rather like nonsense. When I talk to Mrs. Freere, she says I am morbid, and read too many of those dreadful books. The library is full of them. She won't even look at one. But she is so strong and so clever, I can't wonder at her refusing to be the slave of any feeling not perfectly explicable. And what I feel, and what I know Nancette feels, is not explicable.

If you see that woman again, would you have courage to ask her why she persecutes Nancette like this ? Whether anything could induce her to release the poor girl from her horrible influence ? I think we would do any-thing—sacrifice anything, to have her cured.

Let me know if you like the books I told you to read. I suppose you can get them from the library. I cannot tell you anything about your grandfather, as I have not gone back to school this term, and Stewart is such a lazy beggar at writing letters.

Your affectionate friend,

BASIL.

LETTER II.—FROM LÉONIE ST. JEAN TO BASIL

GLENDENNING.

DEAR BASIL,

You do seem in a changed state of mind. I can hardly figure to myself you, the wild schoolboy, buried in that dull, gloomy Owl's Roost, and with only books (such books!) for company; and that poor reasonless Madame Nancye as a friend. But then I forget Mrs. Freere. She will be able to keep you straight, I hope—I mean, of course, in your senses, for you seem in a fair way of losing them too.

Yes; I have read some of those books. They are more than strange. But I have learnt more even than they can tell me. I have seen the Woman in Black again. Not only seen her, but talked with her. What say you, *mon ami*, to that?

This, then, is how it happened. I was at L'Erée this time, near the old cromlech. She appeared just as suddenly as before. But this time I was not so frightened. She looked ill and haggard, and more sad than wild. We looked at each other for a moment; then I spoke.

'I am glad to see you,' I said. 'I want to ask you some questions.'

She seemed surprised, but she said simply:

'Proceed.'

I took a seat on a broken fragment of the cromlech. I looked full at her, but my heart, I confess, was beating very quickly.

'In the first place,' I said, 'who are you?'

For a moment her eyes flamed. I thought she would have struck me for my temerity. But presently her anger died out. She said in a low, mournful voice :

‘ I was of earth once, but my base passions murdered the womanhood within me. I am now only a force of concentrated evil. I hate the happy, the pure, the good. I tread a path of darkness from which there is no escape. I know the secrets of life and death —my will can traverse space and read the mysteries of the stars and the powers that rule mankind. I withdrew myself from the world. My real self has been dead these many years. I live alone. My needs are few and easily supplied. The elements have no power against me, since I have ceased to be mortal. I come and go as I will—by my will. That is what I am. Are you satisfied ?’

I was not satisfied. I thought she was talking wild nonsense. Perhaps she read my thoughts. I do not know, only suddenly she flamed out :

'You do not believe ! Then why do you yourself pursue these studies ? Why have you pored over the doctrines and theories that first led me astray ? For such knowledge brings its own penalty. The thirst of the spirit cannot be quenched once the fever "to know" is fired in its essence. It goes on, and on, and on. Its ambition becomes infinite, its desires insatiable. It would be as the Being whom it dimly worships, and dimly pursues.'

'And,' I asked, awestruck, 'are you not alive ?'

'Alive !' she said ; her eyes drooped, her voice sank to a murmur. 'What is life ?' she went on dreamily. 'A series of forces —currents set afloat in a miserable bodily frame. I cast it from me long ago.'

Then she seemed to sink down on the rough block of stone. Her black draperies

floated around her. Her head, with its
gleaming snow-white hair, dropped upon
her arms. Crouched there in that strange
attitude, she looked so weird and terrible
that I felt a faint thrill of alarm. Mastering
it, however, by a strong effort, and now
awakened to a full and vivid interest in this
singular being, I again addressed her.

'Will you tell me,' I said, 'anything about
your life on earth ?'

She shuddered convulsively.

'Not now,' she moaned; 'not now. It is
all dark, horrible, torturing. There was only
one ray of light in it, but I lost that—I lost
that.'

Then she threw up her arms in a paroxysm
of despair.

'Oh, my little child !' she cried, in a voice
that thrilled to my very heart. 'My little
child !'

Then I began to perceive that the poor
mystic was, after all, only a mortal, that

keen and fresh in her nature was the mother-
woe of womanhood. Sorrow had doubtless
driven her mad, or learning, or perhaps both.

I murmured some words of pity. My
voice seemed to soothe her. She looked
up at me; her eyes were calm and almost
gentle. She held out both her hands as if
entreating me to come to her. But I shrank
back. That movement of involuntary repul-
sion seemed to turn her once more into the
weird terrible creature I had first seen. She
turned away without a word; again she
seemed to melt into the dusk and dimness of
the falling night. I was alone.

Basil, I am determined, for my sake as
well as yours, to solve this mystery—to
discover the real nature and secret of this
strange being. She is a reality, of that
I am convinced. I no longer feel afraid.

Your faithful friend,

Léonie.

LETTER III.—BASIL GLENDENNING TO LÉONIE ST. JEAN.

DEAR LÉONIE,

Your last letter has put me into a state of excitement. It seems to me that you are destined to help us out of our difficulties. I have come to your opinion about the mind of this woman. I am sure she is mad. How does she live? Where does she procure food, or how manage to get from one of the islands to another? Do any of the people about Guernsey know her? I wish you could ascertain.

Nancette is no better. She always knows when a letter comes from you, and I daren't read it in her presence, it disturbs her so. Is it not strange we have heard nothing of my guardian all this time? I can't imagine where he can be. Have you seen Captain Bec, and is the steamer still loafing about? It is awfully dreary here. You may well talk about my being changed. What with

worry, and anxiety, and perplexity, I sometimes feel as if I, too, should go off my head.
Tell me anything you can discover about the
Woman in Black (sounds a bit like Wilkie
Collins—doesn't it?). A great deal depends
on her. Does she know where Nancette
is? ·With her remarkable powers I should .
reasonably suppose we could not keep that
fact a secret.

What do you think Mrs. Freere said the
other day? I had been talking to her ever
so long about these matters, and thought I
had made an impression. 'My dear boy,'
she said, 'I think hydrophobia is developing
itself in you in a new form!' There!

Affectionately yours,

BASIL GLENDENNING.

LETTER IV.—LÉONIE ST. JEAN TO BASIL GLEN-
DENNING.

DEAR BASIL,

I have seen Captain Bec. He has
had no news of your guardian, and the

steamer lies idle at St. Peter Port, awaiting
his return, or his instructions. I met our
mysterious friend the other night. I took
courage to ask her where she was staying,
but received only the unintelligible answer,
' Where there is air and water.' I asked
our old servant, Jeannette, about her. · She
has lived in Guernsey nearly sixty years, and
knows everything and everyone here. But
she only crossed herself, and said no good
came of inquiring into mysteries that apper-
tain to the Evil One ! I can get no information about this woman except that she is
some uncanny, lonely creature, dwelling by
herself in a cave on one of those desolate
islands beyond or about Chaussey. She
sometimes visits one of the larger islands for
provisions or other purchases, and has a boat
of her own which will live in any storm, so
they say, but bodes ill to the sailor or fisherman who sees it in any weather. You know
how the people here are superstitious ; in fact,

when I ask a question it is enough to scare
them ! I can only be patient, and wait for
my mysterious friend's own confidence. I
grieve to hear your Lady Nancye is no
better. As for you, I say only, take care ;
meddle not too deeply with these dark, un-
wholesome mysteries. No good will come of
it. You are young, *mon ami*, and this life is
not wholesome or good for you. It would
be better could you be the wild schoolboy of
old days. To me it seems there is only one
thing that could put us all right once more
—the return of your guardian. You at Owl's
Roost are apparently becoming gloomy, nervous, depressed. Even your bright, clever
Mrs. Freere is not the same. I, too, find
myself troubled and absorbed. This woman
haunts me. Her presence seems constantly
about, yet I seldom see it. When I do, I
am left more troubled and perplexed. Yet,
believe me, what I can do for you I will. I
am sorry I have no more to tell. She

seems fierce, restless, and uncertain. I must wait.

Your sincere friend,

Léonie.

LETTER V.

Dear Léonie,

Something must be done, and soon, or Nancette will be hopelessly insane ! Lately she gets worse. She sits silent for hours, brooding and melancholy, so that it makes one's heart ache to see her. Mrs. Freere is terribly alarmed. She does not like to call in a doctor for fear he should insist upon her being removed, and in the state of her nerves and general health it would be an awful risk to send her among strangers, however kind or well-disposed they might be. Oh, Léonie, can't you help us ? You are strong, and courageous, and clever. Bring your arts to bear on this terrible being whose influence has been so baneful. See if she is not assail-

able by any means. For I am absolutely
certain that it is *her* power that so
affects Nancette. I tell you she knows
when a letter comes from you if that letter
contains any news of the Woman. It is
singular, but it is perfectly true. I am most
unhappy—so is Mrs. Freere. I would run
the risk of having that dreadful creature
over here, if she would promise to cure Nancette of her strange hallucination. Is she
persuadable, do you think? I would fetch
or meet her, and we could get to Owl's Roost
unobserved. Desperate cases want desperate
remedies, you know. Pray write as soon as
you can, and let me know if you can do anything to help us. Most of the servants have
left. Old Clitheroe is dying, and a report
has got about that Owl's Roost is haunted.
Imagine how lively all this is for me and
poor Mrs. Freere!

Yours, always affectionately,

BASIL.

LETTER VI.

DEAR BASIL,

It is a week since I had your letter.
What will you say when I tell you that I
fear the slight hold I had on this strange
woman has snapped — that in my own
opinion I do not fancy I shall ever see her
again ? I hardly know how to explain. It
is so odd, and yet it all happened. I will
describe it—exact. I sought her each day
for three days. In vain. I could hear
nothing, see nothing of her. The fourth,
quite suddenly, she came to me by the sea.
Rain had been falling all day. The air
was chill, and damp, and misty. She seemed
to step out of the shadows herself, with her
dark, sweeping garments, and her strange,
gleaming hair. I started, but I went forward to welcome her, full only of your letter
and its urgent wishes. We said a few words,
then I put my hand in my pocket and drew

out the letter, as I thought. I wanted to
refer to something. There was light enough
to see the writing, and I spread it open; but
as my eye fell on it I saw I had made a
mistake. The letter was from my father. I
had received it that morning. I began to
replace it in the envelope when suddenly the
woman seized my arm with her cold, steel-
like fingers. Her eyes were fixed on the
letter. She looked like a demon—so wild,
so enraged, so awful.

'Who writes to you like that?' she hissed
in my ear. 'Is he lover or friend?'

I was so alarmed at her face, her voice,
her furious words, that I could scarcely
speak. At last I said:

'The letter is only from my father,
madame.'

She gave a low, strange cry; she released
my arm; she stood a few paces off, trembling in every limb. I was too startled

for speech. I only stood still and watched her.

'Your—father!' she said at last. 'And what is the name of your father?'

'Pierre St. Jean,' I answered in surprise.

She shook her head.

'A lie!' she said. 'His lie, and you repeat it.'

'Madame!' I stammered in amaze.

Her imperious hand silenced me.

'What is your name?' she asked, her voice low and fierce, with something in its tones that reminded me of the throb of the sea, its passionate pulses held in check before a coming storm.

'My name,' I said, 'is Léonie.'

Then she gave a low, strange cry, as of some dumb creature in pain, and tossed her wild arms upwards to the stormy sky, and, hissing out a curse that seemed to chill and terrify me, she flew like a wild, hunted thing along

the shore and was lost to sight in a moment.
I stood there, cold, and trembling, and full of
wonder. She did not come back, and at last
I turned homewards. As I stood on the
cliff before turning inland, I saw a boat with
a red sail speeding swiftly over the rough
wild waters. The clouds were rent and
scattered; the light of the stormy sunset
poured itself over the sea. The boat flew on
like a bird, mounting the waves, or plunging
fearlessly into the grim trough of the divid-
ing waters. I watched it with a sort of
wonder. It was no night for a boat to be
out; storm and darkness were already brooding over sea and land. Suddenly I heard a
voice beside me saying: 'It is the witch's
boat. Heaven have mercy on the souls
that meet it!' I looked round. I saw a
fisherman standing there, his eyes fixed on
the little vessel as it scudded fearlessly along.
I did not speak. I only watched it with a
sort of horror and wonder. Then the red

light faded out of the sky. Darkness swept
down like a thick cloud. The wind arose,
and blew in swift, fierce gusts over the face
of the cliffs, and I heard the screams of the
cormorants and gulls as they whirled and
circled round the rocks below.

Then I ran swiftly home through the
rain and the mist, conscious—why I could
not say—that the weird woman had returned to her own home in the deserted
island; that I was powerless to assist you
now.

I have waited till the end of the week.
She has not been here again. Sometimes I
think her boat could not have lived through
that storm, but they say her power is super-
natural. I cannot tell. This only I know
—that though but a few miles of sea separate
us, I am powerless to reach her, or communi-
cate with her. So, *mon ami*, I send this
letter with a heavy heart and many regrets.